THE DEADLY DANCE

THE DEADLY DANCE

†

M. C. BEATON

ST. MARTIN'S MINOTAUR
NEW YORK

ISBN 0-312-30436-6

For Richard Rasdall of Stow-on-the Wold,
his wife, Lyn, and children, Luke, Samuel and Bethany,
and with many thanks to Richard for freeing up Agatha's brain

ONE

†

THE thing that finally nudged Agatha Raisin into opening her own detective agency was what she always thought of as the Paris Incident.

Made restless by the summer torpor blanketing the village of Carsely in the Cotswolds, Agatha decided to take a week's holiday in Paris.

She was a rich woman, but like all rich people was occasionally struck by periods of thrift, and so she had booked into a small hotel off Saint Germain des Prés in the Latin Quarter. She had visited Paris before and seen all the sights; this time wanted only to sit in cafés and watch the people go by or take long walks by the Seine.

But Paris, after the first two days, became even hotter than Carsely and her hotel room did not have any air-conditioning. As the heat mounted to 105 degrees Fahrenheit and she tossed and turned on her damp sheets, she discovered that Paris never sleeps. There were two restaurants across the road with outside tables, and, up until one in the morning, the accordion players came around to get money from the diners. Agatha, as she listened to another rendering of "La Vie en Rose," fantasized about lobbing a hand grenade through the window. Then there was the roar of the traffic and the yells of the tourists who had drunk not too wisely. Later on, as they felt not too well, she could hear moans and retching.

Nonetheless, she decided to see as much of Paris as possible. The Métro was cheap and went all over the place.

On the fourth day of her visit, she went down into the Métro at Maubert-Mutualité. She sat down on a hard plastic seat on the platform and pulled out her subway map. She planned to go to W. H. Smith on the Rue de Rivoli and buy some English books.

As she heard the train approaching, she stuffed the map back in her handbag, flipped open the doors of the carriage with that silver handle which had so bemused her when she had first tried to board, and went inside, aware that someone was crowding behind her, and at the same time feeling a sort of tremor reverberating from her handbag up through the shoulder strap.

She glanced down and saw that her handbag was open again and that her wallet was missing.

Agatha stared wrathfully at the man who had crowded behind her. He was of medium height, white, with black hair, wearing a blue shirt and blue jeans.

"Here, you!" Agatha advanced on him. He nipped out of the carriage and into the next one, with Agatha in pursuit. Just as she was leaning forward to grab him and the train was moving out, he wrenched open the doors of the carriage and escaped onto the platform, leaving Agatha, who did not have the strength to do the same thing, being carried furiously away to the next station.

Agatha blamed the hairdresser. A Parisian hairdresser had told her that there was no crime around Maubert because of the huge commissariat. So Agatha took the Métro back to Maubert, darted up the escalator and demanded directions to the commissariat. She was told it was just round the corner.

It was an ugly modern building with steep steps up to the main entrance. Dripping with sweat and bad temper, Agatha erupted into the entrance hall. There was a very beautiful girl with long dark hair sitting behind bulletproof glass.

Agatha poured out her tale of the mugging, expecting to be shown to some detective's room immediately, but the girl began to interview her. Agatha thought sourly that someone so young and attractive should give way to someone with a bit more authority.

She was fortunate in that she had only had sixty euros in her wallet and that she had left her credit cards in the hotel safe. Her passport was in another compartment of her bag.

After she had been interviewed and had handed over her passport, she was told to take a seat and wait.

"Why don't you have air-conditioning in this place?" she grumbled, but the beautiful girl merely smiled at her benignly.

At last a tall policeman came out and led her into a side room. He sat down behind a desk and waved her into a chair opposite. He looked like those illustrations of Don Quixote of La Mancha. Once more, she described the mugger in detail, ending with "Paris is crawling with gendarmes. Why don't you get down the Métro and catch thieves?"

"We do, every day," he said calmly in perfect English.

"I myself am a detective," said Agatha grandly.

"Indeed!" said Don Quixote, showing a glimmer of interest. "To which police station in England are you attached?"

"I'm not. I mean, I'm going to open my own detective agency."

The flicker of interest died. "Wait here," he said.

There was a mirror behind his desk. Agatha rose and stared at her face in it. She was bright red with heat and her normally glossy brown hair was damp and limp.

Agatha sat down again as he re-entered the room with a typed letter for her to sign. All in French.

"What's this about?" demanded Agatha.

"It is for your insurance and states that if we catch him, he will receive three years in prison and a fine of three thousand euros. If we find your wallet it will be sent to the British Embassy. Sign here."

Agatha signed.

"That will be all."

"Wait a minute. What about mug shots?"

"Please?"

"Photographs of criminals. I'd know that bastard anywhere."

"Three other people have had goods stolen this morning by the same man. They are French. There is no need for your services."

Wrathfully, Agatha got to her feet. "I could do a better job than you any day."

He gave a faint, uninterested sort of smile. "Then I wish you luck."

Agatha went straight back to her hotel and checked out. She was going home and she was going to start her own detective agency.

She had been dithering about it for weeks, but the theft of her wallet had left her with a feeling of not being in charge of events. Agatha Raisin liked to be in charge of everything.

At Charles de Gaulle Airport, she was just heading for the gate but ran into a crowd of people being held back by police. "What's happening?" she asked a man next to her.

"Someone's left a suitcase or package unattended."

Agatha waited, fuming. Then there was a huge blast. From the chatter around her, she gathered that they had blown up whatever it was with a controlled explosion. At Heathrow or other airports they might appeal to the owners to come and claim their suitcase or package, but in France it seemed that they just went ahead and blew it up.

As Agatha drove from Heathrow, black clouds began to pile up in the sky and by the time she turned down the road to Carsely, the countryside was rocking and rolling under the blows of a tremendous thunderstorm.

Agatha's two cats, Hodge and Boswell, came to meet her when she opened the door. Her cleaner, Doris Simpson, came round every day while Agatha was away to feed the cats and let them in and out of the garden.

Agatha dumped her suitcase in the hall and went through to the kitchen and opened the back door. Rain poured down from the thatch overhead, but the air was cool and sweet. Anxious not to lose her determination to set up her own detective agency, Agatha decided to visit her friend, Mrs. Bloxby, the vicar's wife.

Ten minutes later, Agatha rang the bell of the vicarage with a guilty feeling that she should have phoned first.

But Mrs. Bloxby answered the door, her gentle features

lighting up in a smile of welcome. "Mrs. Raisin! How nice. Come in. Why are you back early?"

"I got mugged," said Agatha. She recounted her adventure.

"Well, you got pickpocketed," corrected Mrs. Bloxby mildly. "Unlike you to let something like that put you off Paris. I thought you loved Paris."

"I do, most of the time," fretted Agatha. "It was mainly the heat and the lack of sleep. And being dismissed by the police, just like that! The trouble is they spend all their time policing demonstrations, they haven't got time for the public."

"You don't know that."

"Anyway, it gave me the jolt I needed to start my own agency. You do think it's a good idea, don't you?"

"Oh, yes," agreed Mrs. Bloxby. Although she thought the work would be dreary and sordid, it would occupy her friend's restless mind and keep her from falling in love again and getting hurt. Agatha was addicted to falling in love.

"I've been thinking about starting a detective agency for a time," said Agatha. "I feel I need some official status. I'm a good businesswoman and I feel sure I could make it work. The police are so busy these days and the countryside police stations have been closed one after the other. The police haven't got time for small burglaries, missing teenagers, or errant wives and husbands."

"And if it doesn't work out?" asked the vicar's wife.

Agatha grinned. "I'll take it off my taxes. Anyone taken James's cottage?"

It had not been Agatha's ex-husband James Lacey's cottage for some time, but Agatha always dreamt that one day he would come back to the village. She could never think of that cottage next to her own as belonging to anyone else. Agatha had fallen in love with two of the previous owners.

"Yes, as a matter of fact. A Mrs. Emma Comfrey, retired civil servant. You should call on her."

"Maybe. But I've got a lot to do. I'll go to the estate agent's in Mircester tomorrow and see what's on offer in the way of an office."

Mrs. Bloxby reflected ruefully that Agatha's interest in her new neighbour had died as soon as she found out it was a woman, and a retired one at that.

It took much more money to set up a detective agency than Agatha ever dreamt it would. Brought up on Raymond Chandler–type movies, she had assumed that one sat in an office and waited for the beautiful dame with the shoulder pads to come swaying in—or something like that.

She quickly found out by surfing the net that detective agencies were supposed to offer a wide range of services, including all sorts of modern technology such as bugging and de-bugging, photographic or video evidence and covert and electronic surveillance.

Then someone would be needed to man the phones while she was out of the office. Agatha was shrewd enough to know now that one-woman operations were for novels. She would need to invest heavily in employing experts if she expected to get any return.

Once she had found an office in the centre of Mircester, she put advertisements in the local newspapers. For the photographic and video evidence, she hired a retired provincial newspaper photographer, Sammy Allen, arranging to pay him on a free-lance basis; and she secured the services of a retired police technician, Douglas Ballantine, under the same terms to cope with the electronic stuff.

But for a secretary, Agatha wanted someone intelligent who would be able to detect as well.

She began to despair. The applicants were very young and all seemed to be decorated with various piercings and tattoos.

Agatha was just wondering whether she should try to do any secretarial work herself when there came a knock at the door of the office. The door did not have a pane of frosted glass, which Agatha would have found more in keeping with the old-fashioned idea she had of detective agencies.

"Come in," she shouted, wondering if this could be her first client.

A very tall, thin woman entered. She had thick grey hair, cut short, a long thin face and sharp brown eyes. Her teeth were very large and strong. Her hands and feet were very large, the feet encased in sturdy walking shoes, and the hands were ringless. She was wearing a tweed suit which looked as if she had had it for years.

"Please sit down," said Agatha. "May I offer you some tea? Coffee?"

"Coffee, please. Two sugars, no milk."

Agatha went over to the new coffee machine and poured a mug, added two spoonfuls of sugar and placed it on the desk in front of what she hopefully thought was her first client.

Agatha was a well-preserved woman in her early fifties with short, shining brown hair, a good mouth and small bearlike eyes which looked suspiciously out at the world. Her figure was stocky, but her legs were her finest feature.

"I am Mrs. Emma Comfrey."

Agatha wondered for a moment why the name was familiar and then she remembered that Mrs. Comfrey was her new neighbour.

Agatha found it hard to smile spontaneously but she bared her teeth in what she hoped was a friendly welcome. "And what is your problem?"

"I saw your advertisement in the newspapers. For a secretary. I am applying for the job."

Mrs. Comfrey's voice was clear, well-enunciated, upper-class. Agatha's working-class soul gave a brief twinge and she said harshly, "I would expect any secretary to help with the detective side if necessary. For that I would need someone young and active."

Her eyes bored into Mrs. Comfrey's thin face and flicked down her long figure.

"I am obviously not young," said Mrs. Comfrey, "but I am active, computer-literate, and have a pleasant phone manner which you might find helps."

"How old are you?"

"Sixty-seven."

"Dear God."

"But very intelligent," said Mrs. Comfrey.

Agatha sighed, and was about to tell her to get lost when there came a timid knock at the door.

"Come in," called Agatha.

A harassed-looking woman entered. "I need a detective," she said.

Mrs. Comfrey took her coffee and moved over to a sofa at the side of the office.

Vowing to get rid of Emma as soon as they were alone again, Agatha asked, "What can I do for you?"

"My Bertie has been missing for a whole day now."

"How old is Bertie?"

"Seven."

"Have you been to the police? Silly question. Of course you must have been to the police."

"They weren't interested," she wailed. She was wearing black leggings and a faded black T-shirt. Her hair was blonde but showing dark at the roots. "My name is Mrs. Evans."

"I fail to see . . ." Agatha was beginning when Emma said, "Bertie is your cat, isn't he?"

Mrs. Evans swung round.

"Oh, yes. And he's never run away before."

"Do you have a photograph?" asked Emma.

Mrs. Evans fumbled in a battered handbag and took out a little stack of photographs. "That's the best one," she said, standing up and handing a photograph of a black-and-white cat to Emma. "It was taken in our garden."

She sat down beside Emma, who put a comforting arm around her shoulders. "Don't worry. We'll find your cat."

"How much will it cost?" asked Mrs. Evans.

Agatha had a list of charges but that list did not include finding stray cats.

"Fifty pounds plus expenses if we find him," said Emma. "I am Mrs. Raisin's secretary. If you will just give me your full name and address and telephone number."

Numbly Agatha handed Emma a notebook. Emma wrote down the particulars.

"Now, you go on home," said Emma, helping her to her feet, "and don't worry about a thing. If Bertie can be found, we'll find him."

When the door closed behind a grateful Mrs. Evans, Agatha said, "You're rather high-handed, but here's what I'll do. Find that cat and you've got a job."

"Very well," said Emma calmly, tucking the notebook into her capacious handbag. "Thank you for the coffee."

And that'll be the last I'll hear from her, thought Agatha.

Emma Comfrey checked the address in the notebook. She went into a pet shop nearby and bought a cat carrier and asked for a receipt. Mrs. Evans lived on a housing estate on the outskirts of Mircester. Emma tucked herself into her small Ford Escort and drove out to the housing estate. She noticed that Mrs. Evans lived in a row of houses whose back gardens bordered farmland. The farmers had been getting the harvest in and Emma knew that meant lots of field mice for a cat to chase.

She parked the car and made her way to a path that led to the fields. She walked into the first field, her sensible shoes treading through the stubble. The day was warm and pleasant, with little feathery wisps of cloud on a pale blue sky. Emma studied the field and then looked back to where the Evanses' back garden was located. There were a bordering of gorse bushes and tall grass at the edge of the field. She made her way there and suddenly sat down on the ground, feeling rather shaky. She could not believe now that she'd had the temerity to ask for the job, and felt sure there was no hope of finding the cat.

Emma had been married in her early twenties to a barrister,

Joseph Comfrey. He had a good income, but barely three weeks after the honeymoon, he said that it was bad for Emma to sit around the house and she should get work. Emma, an only child, had been bullied by her parents, and so she had meekly taken the Civil Service exams and settled into boring secretarial work for the Ministry of Defence. Joseph was mean. Although he spent quite a lot on himself—the latest Jaguar, shirts from Jermyn Street and suits from Savile Row—he took control of Emma's wages and only gave her a small allowance. When she retired, he grumbled day in and day out about the paucity of her pension. Two years ago he had died of a heart attack, leaving Emma a very wealthy woman. She did not have any children; Joseph did not approve of children. At first she had spent long days and nights alone in their large villa in Barnes. The habits of strict economy forced on her by her husband were hard to break. She could still hear his nagging, hectoring voice haunting the rooms.

At last she found courage to sell the house. She packed up her husband's clothes and gave them to charity. She presented his law books to an aspiring barrister and bought the cottage in Lilac Lane next to Agatha's. Although the women in the village were friendly, she became interested in the stories she heard about her next-door neighbour and then she saw Agatha's advertisement for a secretary. Time was lying heavy on her hands. It took a great deal of courage to walk into Agatha's office and ask for the job. Had Agatha been less pugnacious, the normally timid Emma might have apologized her way out of any chance of securing the post, but Agatha's manner brought forcibly to Emma's mind her bullying husband and various nasty people she had worked with over the years and that had given her courage.

Emma sighed. Her little moment of glory was over. The wretched cat could be anywhere: picked up as a stray, flattened by a truck. Emma had been brought up as a Methodist, but gradually she had ceased to attend the services. She still believed vaguely that there must be a power for good in the universe. She sat for a long time, hugging her bony knees and watching cloud shadows chase each other across the golden stubble. She suddenly felt at peace, as if the past and its miseries and the future and its uncertainties had all been wiped from her mind. At last she rose and stretched. Time to go through the motions of looking for the cat.

Just as she was turning away, a shaft of sunlight struck down on the tall grass and gorse bushes and she caught a glimpse of something. She parted the grass and peered down. A black-and-white cat was lying fast asleep.

Emma went quietly back to the car and got the cat box and returned, hoping against hope that the cat was still there. Her luck held. She bent down and caught the cat by the scruff and popped it in the box. She looked at the houses and at the Evanses's house in particular. No one in sight.

"First bit of luck I've had in my life," said Emma. "Just wait until that Raisin female sees this!"

Agatha looked up hopefully as the door of the office opened, and her face fell when she saw Emma. And then she saw the cat carrier. "Good heavens! Is that Bertie?"

"Indeed it is."

"Are you sure?"

"I found him in a field at the back of his home. I've checked with the photographs. I have a receipt for the carrier and I will need to buy cat food and a litter tray and litter."

"Why on earth? I mean, phone the woman up and get her here."

"Not a good idea."

"May I remind you who's boss here?"

"Listen. Would it not be better to wait until this evening? Don't want to make it look too easy. Tell her we found Bertie wandering on the motorway and saved his life. Then I'll phone the *Mircester Journal* and give them a cosy story about the new detective agency."

Agatha, who had never been outclassed when it came to public relations before, felt a stab of jealousy. As Agatha never recognized jealousy in herself, she put it down to too much coffee.

"Very well," she said gruffly.

"So I've got the job?"

"Yes."

Emma smiled happily. "I'll just get the necessary for the cat and then we can discuss my wages."

The *Mircester Journal* knew that happy stories were what really sold the paper. After some discussion, Emma and Agatha decided to keep the cat in the office overnight, present it to Mrs. Evans first thing in the morning and make sure a reporter and photographer were present.

Emma could barely sleep. She had visions of Bertie dying in the night and of one of Mrs. Evans's neighbours coming forward to say that she had seen a woman snatching the cat out of the field the day before.

But everything went amazingly smoothly. Agatha longed to

take all the credit but could hardly claim any with Emma standing there. She felt quite sulky when the *Mircester Journal* used a photograph of Mrs. Evans, Emma and the cat, but did mention the new detective agency.

TWO

†

AFTER a week of working—or rather barely working—for Agatha, Emma could feel the little personality she had found for herself crumbling away bit by bit. Agatha was very much the boss. She had instructed Emma to prepare computer files for all the cases she hoped to get. Other than that, she barely spoke to her, and in the evening they went off in their respective cars to Carsely.

Agatha was cross that the first publicity for the new agency had given praise to Emma. The photographer had taken a photo of Agatha and she had worn her new power suit especially for the occasion, but that photograph had not been used.

Of course she told everyone in the village who asked that she was lucky to have "found" Emma. Only Mrs. Bloxby was not deceived.

Agatha had chosen an office in one of the old medieval lanes of central Mircester. It was situated above an antique shop. Now she wished she had gone for a cheaper place, perhaps out in the industrial estate. She felt tucked away and it was impossible for anyone to park outside.

After two weeks, Agatha felt she had good reason to sack Emma. It was silly to pay wages to a secretary who had no work to do.

She braced herself, looking truculently at Emma, who was immersed in a book. Agatha coughed. Emma looked up. She knew the chop was coming and her heart sank.

And then they both heard the voice of Dennis Burley, the antique dealer, saying, "Yes, go on right up. The agency's on your right at the first landing."

Both women looked at each other, momentarily bonded by hope.

A small man wearing a flat cap, a polo shirt and baggy flannels came in without knocking. His face seemed to be all nose, as if some godly hand had pulled his face forward at birth. A small toothbrush moustache lurked under its shadow.

"Please sit down," cooed Agatha. "Tea or coffee?"

He cleared his throat. "Nothing. I wonder if you can help me."

Emma produced her notebook.

"My son has gone missing," he said.

"May I have your name?"

"I'm Harry Johnson. My son is called Wayne. He's nineteen."

"Have you been to the police?"

"Yes, but Wayne's got a bit of a record for stealing cars, so they're not bothering much."

"How long has he been missing?"

"Two days."

"Does he normally live with you?"

"Yes; here's my card."

He extracted his wallet and fished out a card. Emma rose and took it from him, noting that Mr. Johnson was a plumber.

"Can you give us a list of places he usually frequents?"

"He likes going to Poppy's Disco, reckon pretty much all the pubs, that's about all."

Emma suddenly spoke. "Mr. Johnson, why are you so anxious about him? He is nineteen, he likes pubs and clubs. Might he not just have taken off somewhere? Does he have a car?"

"Yes, he does. My bleedin' car. That's why I want to find him."

"Make of car and registration?" asked Emma, while Agatha fretted. *She* should be the one asking all the questions.

"It's a red Rover SL-44. Here. I'll write down the registration number for you."

"Quite an old car," said Emma.

"But I kept it beautiful. I told him he was never to touch it. He must have taken the keys off the table while I was asleep in front of the telly. How much do you lot charge?"

"If we recover your car, the charge will be a hundred pounds," said Emma, "but our expenses will be added on. They may not amount to much unless he has gone out of town."

"I'm not a rich man," said Mr. Johnson. "Oh, go ahead. But I don't want to be running up no big expenses. If you haven't found him after two days, forget it."

"I'll get you the form to sign," said Emma, going to a filing cabinet. Agatha's eyes narrowed. She didn't even know they had a suitable form. Also, Emma was no longer wearing the old tweed suit but a smart linen skirt and blouse. I hope the cow isn't thinking of taking over, thought Agatha sourly.

"Here we are," said Emma. "I'll fill in the money—here—and then you sign here and here. Fill in your address and your phone numbers and an e-mail address if you have it. If you will give us a cheque for a hundred pounds now, then we will bill you for any expenses."

He brought out a battered wallet. "Credit card?"

"No," said Emma with a smile. "Cheque and bank card, please. Oh, and we'll need a photograph."

He took a photograph from his inside pocket and was about to hand it to Emma, but Emma, conscious of Agatha's eyes boring into her, said, "Please hand it to Mrs. Raisin."

Agatha looked down at the photograph in surprise. "This is your car. Haven't you got a photograph of your son?"

"Oh, him. Yeah, got one here." He ferreted back in his inside pocket and produced a small passport photo.

Wayne had black hair gelled up into a crest on top of his head. He had a nose stud and five little earrings in one ear. His face was thin and his lips were curled in a sneer.

"Do I get my money back if you don't find my car . . . I mean, him?" asked Mr. Johnson.

Agatha looked at Emma. "No, but you will not be charged expenses," said Emma.

"Right, I'll be on me way. Keep me posted."

There was a silence after he had left, and then Agatha said, "We didn't charge enough. The rent of this place is awful, not to mention the business tax."

"I thought it might be an idea to keep prices low until we have built up a reputation."

"In future, consult me. Right? Now, I'd better get started."

"Do you want me to go and look for the boy?" asked Emma.

"Remember this. You're a secretary. So stay here and man the phones."

Agatha went straight to Mircester Police Headquarters and asked to speak to her friend, Detective Sergeant Bill Wong. She was in luck; Bill was not out on a case.

"I'm sorry I haven't been round to see you," said Bill. "I read in the paper that you'd opened up your detective agency. How's it going? Who is this Emma Comfrey who found the cat?"

"She's only my secretary. She's my new neighbour and wanted the job. Actually, she got lucky, that's all. I'm thinking of replacing her with someone young. I mean, she's sixty-seven, for God's sake." Like a lot of people in their fifties, Agatha considered sixty-something ancient, as if it were an age she would never reach.

"Fit and well?"

"Yes."

"I'd think that'd be an asset, Agatha. I mean, if you're out and about and someone calls, it would be reassuring to have a mature woman there instead of some little girl."

"I think she's too pushy."

Bill roared with laughter. Then he said, "Coming from you, that's rich. Don't glare at me. You want something. What?"

Agatha told him about the missing Wayne.

"Oh, that one," said Bill. "I've picked him up a couple of times for drunk and disorderly. He wasn't driving at the time. Has he got a licence?"

"I didn't check," mumbled Agatha, and then in a stronger voice. "That's Emma's fault. She was the one asking all the questions. I couldn't get a word in edgeways."

"Talking about licences, Agatha. Do you have one for the agency?"

"Don't need one yet in the UK. You should know that. How do I start looking for Wayne?"

"Every pub and club in Mircester. Last time I arrested him was outside Poppy's Disco."

"He's taken his father's Rover and Pa wants that back more than his son. Could you be an angel and run the registration through your computer and see if it's turned up smashed anywhere?"

"Just this once," said Bill severely. "You can't expect me to do all your detecting for you. Wait here."

"As if I hadn't helped you before," grumbled Agatha to his retreating back.

Bill Wong was Agatha's oldest and first friend. When she had sold her public relations business and taken early retirement and moved to the Cotswolds, Bill, son of a Chinese father and Gloucestershire mother, had investigated what Agatha remembered as her first case. Before that, grumpy and prickly Agatha had not had any friends.

While Bill was away, Agatha wondered what to do about Emma Comfrey. Mrs. Bloxby was so pleased she had employed Emma and Agatha did not want to disappoint Mrs. Bloxby, but she regarded Emma as a rival.

While she was waiting, her mobile phone rang. It was Emma.

"Mr. Johnson has just called," she said in those clear upper-class accents which made Agatha feel so diminished. "He says the car has been returned and is outside his house. He says it's all right—no scratches and a full tank of petrol. He tried to cancel the investigation and get his money back, but I told him that it would look extremely bad for him if anything had happened to his son and he had done nothing to find him. So he agreed."

"I'd better get round there," said Agatha.

She rang off just as Bill returned. She told him about the reappearance of the car.

"You're a waste of time, Agatha," said Bill. "But there's one thing I do remember. Wayne had a girl-friend. She hit me with her handbag last time I arrested him."

"What's her name?"

"Sophy Grigson. You'll find her at the check-out at Branford's supermarket in the square."

"Thanks, Bill. I owe you."

Agatha made her way to the supermarket. She asked the manager if she could speak to Sophy Grigson about a missing person. "She'll be on her break in ten minutes," he said.

"I'll wait."

Agatha sat down on one of the hard plastic chairs at the supermarket entrance, placed there for elderly customers.

In ten minutes' time, the manager led a surly, plump girl up to Agatha and said, "Sophy Grigson," and walked off.

"Please sit down, Miss Grigson," said Agatha.

"What's this about then?" Sophy asked, moving a wad of chewing gum from one cheek to the other.

She had blonded hair scraped up on top of her head. Although young, her face was prematurely set in an expression of discontent. "It's about Wayne Johnson."

"Oh, 'im. Bastard."

"He's missing."

" 'E's missing his marbles, that's what."

"Have you seen him recently?"

"Naw. Heard 'e'd gone peculiar."

"What do you mean by that?"

" 'Is pal. Jimmy Swithe, 'e comes in this mornink, and he says, 'You'll never guess what's 'appened to our Wayne.' I asks him what 'e means and 'e starts to talk but the Nazi ower there says, 'You 'ave customers waiting.' Cow!"

"Where can I find Jimmy?"

"At Stonebridge services."

"The petrol station."

"That's it."

Agatha was just leaving the supermarket when her phone rang. Emma again. "Mrs. Raisin," said Emma formally, "I think you should return to the office. We have a client."

Agatha hurried back to the office. An expensively dressed woman was sitting in one of the visitors' chairs, being served coffee by Emma.

"Mrs. Benington," said Emma, "this is our private investigator, Mrs. Raisin."

Everything about Mrs. Benington looked hard, from her lacquered hair to her glittering red nails. She had slightly prominent eyes with heavy lids and a small thin mouth, bright red with the sort of lipstick one paints on with a brush. She was tanned with that sun shower treatment that is supposed to look natural but never does. Her figure under a tailored jacket, blouse and short skirt was very good. Her legs were the thin kind that used to be so admired, ending in shoes that looked as if they had been made from crocodile skin. Surely not in these politically correct days, thought Agatha, although Mrs. Benington, radiating pent-up energy, looked perfectly capable of killing a crocodile herself.

"How can I help you?" asked Agatha.

"I think my husband's cheating on me. I want proof."

"Yes, we can do that for you. As to charges . . . ?"

"Mrs. Comfrey has already discussed the charges with me and I have agreed."

Agatha's eyes narrowed into slits. Emma rushed forward and put a signed agreement in front of Agatha. Agatha was all prepared to blast Emma until she saw that Emma had charged an extraordinarily high amount along with generous expenses.

"Excellent," Agatha forced herself to say.

"I have given Mrs. Comfrey a cheque," said Mrs. Benington, getting to her feet. "I must say, I was reassured. In this nasty business, it is so nice to be dealing with a lady." And she smiled at Emma.

When she had left, Agatha said, "In future, Emma, do not charge any amount of money without consulting me first."

Emma could feel her old crushed self about to whimper out an apology. But she felt she had got this far by pretending to be self-confident and she knew that any sign of weakness and the formidable Agatha would have her by the throat.

"In this case," she said mildly, "what would you have charged?"

Agatha opened her mouth to blast her and then suddenly shut it again. For the first time in her life, she heard a voice in her brain telling her that she was jealous.

She stared for a long moment at Emma and then shrugged. "I really don't know, Emma, but I certainly would not have dreamt of charging so much. Well done. Now, I'd better phone our photographer, Sammy, and also Douglas for surveillance and get them on the job. Would you like to try your hand at some more detective work?"

"You mean the Johnson boy?"

"Yes, him. The father's got his car back as good as new, but there's no sign of Wayne. Wayne has a friend, Jimmy Swithe, who works at Stonebridge petrol station. You could try there first."

Emma's face lit up in a smile. "I'll get on to it right away."

When the door closed behind her tall, thin figure, Agatha Raisin said ruefully, "I am a bitch, that's what I am," and picked up the receiver to start investigating Mrs. Benington's husband.

Emma Comfrey arrived at the petrol station and asked for Jimmy Swithe. She was told he was working on a car in the garage at the side.

Feeling waves of her usual timidity about to engulf her, Emma took a deep breath. I will act as if I am brave, she told herself. A burly man in stained overalls was bent over a car. "Mr. Swithe?"

He jerked his hand towards the back of the garage. Emma walked forwards into the gloom. A young man was sitting on an upturned oil drum under a "No Smoking" sign lighting a cigarette. He had lank brown hair and an unhealthy white face stained with smears of oil.

"Mr. Swithe?"

"Yes." He looked at her with contempt. But then, Emma,

reminded herself sternly, he probably looked with contempt at anyone over twenty-five.

"I am a detective," said Emma.

"What? You? Is this a joke?"

Emma coloured. "I have been employed by Mr. Johnson to find his son, Wayne."

"Don't have nothing to do with him."

"Why?"

"He's gone funny."

"You mean he's become a comedian?"

"Naw. He found religion."

"Which religion?"

"Youth for Jesus Christ."

"And where might I find them?"

"Out the Stow Road on the industrial estate. One o' them old Nissen huts. Can't miss it. They've put a cross on the roof. Wankers!"

Emma thanked him and retreated, already beginning to feel a warm glow of achievement. The first little seed of dislike for Agatha was sown. Previously, Emma had not thought herself worthy of disliking anyone.

She got back in her car and drove off in the direction of the industrial estate. At first she thought she had been misdirected as she circled round and round, but then she suddenly saw a golden cross glittering through a stand of trees on a side road she had not noticed before.

Emma drove up to the Nissen hut, one of those corrugated roofed buildings left over from World War II. She could hear the sound of singing. She got out of the car, went up to the hut and opened the door. It was full of mostly young people singing "All Thing Bright and Beautiful." They were waving their arms in the air and swaying, emulating American Southern Baptist choirs, which was unfortunate, thought Emma, because they lacked the joyful fluidity of movement of the Baptists, their sticklike white arms moving jerkily.

Fortunately, it turned out to be the final hymn. A reedy man with thick glasses who seemed to be the preacher blessed them all.

Emma waited at the door as the congregation shuffled out, slipping the photograph of Wayne out of her handbag.

She nearly missed him because the nose stud and earrings had gone and his hair was newly washed and flopping over his brow, but she took a chance and asked, "Wayne?"

"Who wants to know?"

"Your father. I am a private detective. He has engaged me to find you."

"He doesn't want to find me. The silly old bugger only wanted his car back. He's got it, so that's it."

"Are you going home?"

"No, we got a camp here out the back. It's fun. Tell him I'm okay but I ain't going home. These people look after me like he never did."

Emma fished a camera out of her bag. "May I just take a photograph of you to show him you are well?"

"Sure, go ahead."

Religion had not obviously removed vanity. Wayne lounged against a tree with his hands on his hips and his face turned slightly to one side. "My best side," he said. "If it's any good, let me have a copy."

"This is not one of these strange cults?" said Emma. "I mean, you are free to leave if you want?"

"Any time. No one tells me what to do except God."

Emma decided to call on Mr. Johnson herself. She did not want Agatha to take the credit. Agatha might expect her to hold on to the information a little longer so as to charge for expenses, but then Agatha had not found Wayne—she had.

Mr. Johnson, when told the good news, seemed remarkably underwhelmed. "As long as I've got the car back," he said. "Stupid berk, that boy is. I could have saved myself the money."

Emma felt diminished. Like all bullied people, she often retreated into a fantasy world, and she had built up a picture where Mr. Johnson would fall on her neck, crying with relief, and somehow the local paper would be there to photograph the happy moment.

Agatha was regretting having sent Emma out detecting. She had briefed Sammy Allen and Douglas Ballantine, but she wanted to be out there herself. Emma had taken extensive notes about where Mr. Benington worked, his hobbies, and the make of his car.

She looked up in relief as the door opened and Emma walked in. "Forget about the Johnson boy for the moment," said Agatha. "I've got to go out."

"I found the Johnson boy," said Emma. "I've told the father. I'll bill him for expenses. All he really wanted was his car back."

Agatha experienced a pang of unease. Was she really going to be outclassed by this odd female? Recognizing her own jealousy had upset her. Agatha had always maintained that she hadn't a jealous bone in her body. She glanced at the clock. "Tell you what, it's lunch-time. I think you deserve lunch. It'll do no harm to close up for an hour."

They went to a Chinese restaurant near the agency. Agatha avoided the crispy seaweed, knowing that it had an unfortunate way of sticking to her teeth or finding its way down her clothes.

"Tell me about yourself," said Agatha, determined to be polite, although she wasn't very interested in anything Emma might have to say.

Emma described her work at the Ministry of Defence, making it sound much more glamorous that it had actually been. When Emma had finished, Agatha said, "You've been doing a great job so far. I think we'll make a good team."

After lunch, Emma went back to the office, feeling a warm glow of satisfaction.

Agatha began to feel rather superfluous. Posing as an office phone cleaner, Douglas had bugged Mr. Benington's phone, and Sammy was waiting outside the offices in his car, armed with camera, ready to follow Benington when he left work.

She returned to the office. "I think, as you've proved so useful at detecting," said Agatha, "I may as well hire a girl just to do the phones."

"What about Miss Simms?" asked Emma, referring to Carsely's unmarried mother who was secretary of the ladies' society.

"Hasn't she got a gentleman friend?" asked Agatha.

"I think she's between fellows at the moment. What is her first name? I find it very odd that none of the ladies in the village ever use anyone's first name."

"I think it's Kylie," said Agatha. "It's a tradition. Mrs. Bloxby is a great friend, but I always call her Mrs. Bloxby. Tell you what, you go now and see her. Tell her I'll pay her off the books. No need to get into insurance stamps or social security."

"Isn't that illegal?"

"So what?" said Agatha. "Money is melting away, day in and day out."

Miss Simms, reflected Emma half an hour later, as she sat in the neat living room of Miss Simms's council house, favoured a tarty style of old-fashioned dress. No crop tops or studs. Spiky high heels, long hair dyed blonde, short straight skirt rucked up to show a frilly scarlet petticoat, little white blouse with a black shoelace tie at the neck.

"That's ever so kind of you," said Miss Simms.

"You can type and take shorthand and all that?" asked Emma.

"Oh, yes; computers, too."

"When did you last work?"

Miss Simms creased her smooth brow in thought. "Reckon it was last year. Boss of a soft furnishing business."

"And how long did you work for him?"

Miss Simms giggled. "Just the one day. He said I was too pretty to work and I'd be better off at home so that he could . . . er . . . see me when he wanted."

"And what happened?"

"Just broke up. He was married, see. I don't like to keep the married ones away from their wives for too long. How are you getting along with our Mrs. Raisin?"

"Very well."

"Got a heart of gold," said Miss Simms. "What brought you to Carsely?"

Emma told again her highly embroidered tale, but somehow,

although Miss Simms uttered the occasional "dear me," she did not seem overly impressed. A silly little girl, thought Emma, disappointed. Wish I hadn't recommended her.

When Emma had finished talking, Miss Simms said, "I'll just get a jacket and come into the office with you. May as well find out where everything is."

Agatha fiddled with a paper clip and looked round her new office. There was her own desk, a large pseudo-Georgian affair with two seats in front of it for clients. Against one wall was a sofa facing a low coffee table with neatly arranged magazines. Against the other wall was the desk she had ordered for Emma and two filing cabinets. She had been considering ordering another desk and computer if Miss Simms took the job, but decided it would be better if Miss Simms used Emma's desk and Emma could wait on the sofa.

It was an old building with thick beams on the ceiling and a mullioned window overlooking the narrow street below.

She had placed advertisements for The Raisin Detective Agency—"all calls discreetly dealt with—video and electronic surveillance"—but hardly anyone seemed to be rushing to employ her services.

Agatha heard footsteps on the stairs. That was quick, she thought. It was not Emma or Miss Simms who tapped at the door and walked in, however, but a tall woman who, despite the heat of the day, was wearing a waxed coat over a blouse and tweed skirt, woollen stockings and thick brogues. She had curly brown hair which looked as if she had set it herself in pin-curls. She had very large eyes in a thin face. No make-up.

"I am Mrs. Laggat-Brown," she said, sitting down and facing Agatha across the desk. "I met your friend, Sir Charles Fraith, at a fund-raising event and he told me it would be sensible to apply to you for help."

Agatha had sent Charles a brochure about the new agency. He had not phoned and she had assumed that he was out of the country. She was used to him dropping in and out of her life. They had been lovers—briefly—in the past, but their relationship never seemed to affect him. They had met years ago when Charles had been in danger of being arrested for murder. After that, he had worked with her on some of her cases. He was ten years younger than Agatha and she was very aware of the age difference.

"How can I help you?" asked Agatha.

"You are not quite what I expected," said Mrs. Laggat-Brown in a high, fluting voice.

"What did you expect?"

Mrs. Laggat-Brown had expected someone of "our class," but there was a gleam in Agatha's eyes that stopped her from even implying such a thing.

"Never mind. The situation is this. I live in the manor-house in Herris Cum Magna. Do you know the village?"

"It's off the Stow-Burford Road, isn't it?"

"Yes. Now, listen carefully. I am giving a dinner dance to-morrow for my daughter's twenty-first birthday. My daughter's engagement is to be announced. But my daughter, Cassandra, has received a death threat. She has been told in a letter that if she marries Jason Peterson, she will die. The police have been informed and say they will send two officers to the event."

The door opened and Emma walked in. Agatha introduced them to each other. Mrs. Laggat-Brown surveyed Emma with a flicker of relief in her eyes.

"Sit down, Emma," said Agatha.

Emma sat down. "Miss Simms is shopping. She will be here presently." Emma opened her large handbag and drew out a notebook and pen.

Agatha told Emma what Mrs. Laggat-Brown had just said and then asked, "Can you give us some background on your daughter and this Jason Peterson?"

"Certainly."

It appeared that Jason was a stockbroker from a respectable family. Cassandra had led a sheltered life: Cheltenham Ladies College, followed by a finishing school in Switzerland and then a cordon bleu cookery course in Paris.

The police had the threatening letter.

"Now what I want you to do," said Mrs. Laggat-Brown, "is to come along and mingle with the guests and look for anyone suspicious. I assume you will be dressed as guests."

"Of course." Agatha gave her a frosty look. "Now to our fee."

"I have the cheque here. Sir Charles said I must pay you in advance."

Agatha was about to protest that Sir Charles did not run the agency, but one look at the generous sum on the cheque shut her up. Charles must have quoted the first extravagant price he could think of.

She questioned Mrs. Laggat-Brown further as Emma's pen flew across the pages of her notebook.

According to Mrs. Laggat-Brown, there seemed to be no obvious reason for anyone to want to end the engagement.

Was there a Mr. Laggat-Brown? Not now. They were divorced three years ago, an amicable divorce.

What did Mr. Laggat-Brown do? "He is a stockbroker," said Mrs. Laggat-Brown. "Just like dear Jason."

"Will he be at the party?" asked Agatha.

"He would be if I could find him. His firm said he went on an extended holiday but did not leave an address."

Miss Simms arrived later, carrying shopping bags from various thrift stores. Emma spent the rest of the day instructing her in the files and a new price list she had drawn up.

Agatha was in high excitement at the prospect of what she thought of as a "real" case.

Anxious to tell Mrs. Bloxby about it, no sooner had she arrived home than she fed her cats and let them out in the garden. She reflected that she would have to pay her cleaner, Doris Simpson, something extra to come in during the day and let the cats in and out. Agatha was fond of telling people that she was not an animal lover.

The vicar opened the door to Agatha and gave a thin smile which was not reflected in his eyes. "I'm afraid we are rather busy, Mrs. Raisin . . ." he was beginning to say when Mrs. Bloxby appeared behind him.

"Oh, Mrs. Raisin, do come in," she said over her husband's shoulder. "We'll go into the garden and you can have a cigarette." The vicar muttered something and retreated. A moment later, Agatha heard his study door bang.

"So how is it all going?" asked Mrs. Bloxby when they were seated in the garden.

Agatha told her all that had been happening and about the party the following evening.

"And how is Mrs. Comfrey coping?" asked Mrs. Bloxby.

"Very well. At first I thought that she was too old and pushy."

"Pushy! Mrs. Comfrey!"

"Well, maybe it's a sort of bold front. Seems she had a pretty important job at the ministry."

"Or so she says. I can't imagine her being popular."

"I can't imagine her being unpopular," said Agatha. "She's just too nice. I've hired Miss Simms to be secretary since Emma is doing so well on the detective side."

"And you say Sir Charles recommended you. That was good of him."

"He never comes to see me any more," mourned Agatha.

"He's always been like that, dropping in and out of your life. He'll turn up again. Have you phoned him to thank him?"

"No, I've tried to phone him before, but he was always out or away somewhere."

Before Agatha phoned Charles, she phoned Sammy on his mobile and asked if there had been any progress in the Benington case. "I've got nothing, but Douglas heard one thing he thinks might be it. He's bugged the office as well as the phone."

Agatha repressed a groan, thinking of the expense. "What did he get?"

"Mr. Benington called in his secretary. After dictating letters, very boring stuff, all about clothes and things for their mail-order catalogue, he asked her—her name is Josie—if things were all right for Friday—and she giggled and said okay, that she had told her mum she was off to a business convention. So with any luck it means he's got an assignation for Friday with his secretary."

"Good. Keep on it," said Agatha.

Agatha then phoned Charles. His aunt answered the phone and said Charles was in the bath. "Tell him to call me. Agatha

Raisin," ordered Agatha. The aunt replaced the phone without even saying goodbye. Charles did not phone back.

Probably the old bitch didn't give him the message, thought Agatha, and went upstairs to find a suitable dress to wear for the party.

Mrs. Laggat-Brown was blessed by good weather. A harvest moon was rising above the trees at the manor-house when Agatha and Emma arrived. Fairy lights were strung through the trees and on the lawn was a large striped marquee. A band on the terrace was playing old-fashioned dance numbers. The manor-house itself was one of those low rambling Cotswold stone buildings which are much larger inside than they seem from the outside. Agatha looked around. She and Emma had arrived early, but already there seemed to be a great number of guests arriving. Agatha had compromised by wearing a silk trouser-suit and flat sandals in case there should prove to be any action. Emma was wearing a black satin gown with long sleeves. Agatha thought she looked like a member of the Addams Family, but Mrs. Laggat-Brown, rushing up to greet them, said, "How well you look, Mrs. Comfrey," and to Agatha, "Would you like to go into the house and change?"

Agatha bristled. "I am changed. You cannot expect me to hunt down a potential killer in high heels and a long skirt."

"Oh, very well. The programme is this. The guests will assemble in the marquee, where drinks will be served, followed by dinner. Then they will go outside while the marquee is cleared for dancing. More drinks will be served at the pool house."

"And where is that?" asked Agatha.

"Over at the back of the house, by the swimming pool. I

will announce my daughter's engagement there before the dancing begins."

"Would you like me to search the house?" asked Agatha. "Make sure no one is hiding there?"

"Oh, dear me, no. Some of the guests are there changing and we don't want you poking around, now do we?"

"I thought that was what I was here for," said Agatha.

"Just study the guests and look out for someone who looks as if they don't belong."

"She shouldn't wear a backless dress at her age," said Agatha sourly, watching Mrs. Laggat-Brown retreat. "You can count every single vertebra."

"So where do we start?" asked Emma.

"I don't know about you, but I could do with a large G and T."

"I think it's only champagne," said Emma. "Here comes a girl with a tray."

"Oh, that'll do," grumbled Agatha. She and Emma took a glass each.

"I think that must be Cassandra," said Emma, waving her glass in the direction of the terrace.

Cassandra had masses of sun-streaked hair. She was plump with a round, amiable face. She was wearing a very low-cut dress to show off her best feature—two large round bosoms. Beside her stood a young man in evening dress. He had thick dark hair, a long nose, and a somehow embarrassingly large and red sensual mouth.

A little to the left of them stood a policeman and policewoman.

The guests chatted, the band played, and Agatha's feet began to hurt. And then the guests began to move towards the marquee.

"Great," said Agatha. "Come along, Emma. I'm starving."

Mrs. Laggat-Brown, with her daughter and Jason, had moved to the entrance to the marquee to welcome the guests.

When she saw Agatha and Emma, she said, "We haven't got places for you. If you're very hungry, you can get something in the kitchen."

Agatha wanted to make a scene. She wanted to shout that they were supposed to observe the guests and that she would rather do it sitting down, but reminded herself in time that Mrs. Laggat-Brown was a client and that if she behaved herself this job might lead to others.

Outside, Emma said, "We may as well go to the kitchen."

"Damned if I will," muttered Agatha.

"You see, whoever is working there might have some gossip about the family."

"You're right." But Agatha felt she should have thought of that herself.

THREE

✝

AGATHA had imagined she would find a cook and a maid in the kitchen, forgetting that the days of live-in servants had gone. Mrs. Laggat-Brown had hired a caterer, a formidable-looking woman in jeans and a T-shirt. Agatha explained who they were, ending up asking if there was any supper.

"Sorry," she said briskly. "All in the tent. With people like Mrs. Laggat-Brown, you cater down to the last plate and no more. The girls I've hired for the evening are serving it. I'd take a look in her fridge. There might be something there."

"I don't think we should . . ." began Emma timidly, but Agatha had spotted a chest freezer and a microwave, two essentials in Agatha's opinion for efficient cuisine.

She opened the lid and rummaged through the packets. "Here we are, Emma," she said at last. "Two portions of stew."

Agatha put them in the microwave, turned the knob to defrost, and then heated them up.

"This is not bad," said Agatha when they began to eat. "Got potatoes in it as well."

At last, her appetite satisfied, Agatha turned her attention back to the caterer. "Known Mrs. Laggat-Brown long?"

"No, this is my first job for her and it'll be my last."

"Why is that?"

"Penny-pinching."

"We're detectives," said Agatha. "Her daughter's had a death threat."

"Well, let's just hope they get the old trout instead," said the caterer with a shrug.

"I hope that cheque of hers clears," said Agatha.

"It's all right," said Emma. "I paid the necessary fee to have it cleared quickly."

"Oh, well done!" said Agatha and Emma flushed with pleasure. Really, thought Emma, I think I like her after all.

They made their way back out and located the swimming pool. Stage and microphone had been set up at the pool edge facing the house.

Then they walked back and went into the marquee. Agatha's eyes ranged over the guests. "There can't be anyone here she doesn't know," said Agatha. "No chance of gatecrashers. That one's not going to part with a single extra crumb if she doesn't have to."

Emma's feet in her high heels began to ache and she envied Agatha her flat sandals. "Funny," said Agatha, "if Charles is such a friend of hers, I thought he would have been invited."

At long last the meal was over, and fortunately for the two detectives, the speeches were to be made at the pool.

They went round and took up their positions behind where Mrs. Laggat-Brown would be standing at the microphone.

The guests arrived, laughing and chattering. Agatha had that old lost feeling of being on the outside, looking in.

Mrs. Laggat-Brown, flanked on one side by her daughter and Jason Peterson on the other, stood in front of the microphone. Agatha took up a position directly behind them. Mrs. Laggat-Brown opened her mouth to speak. But from a field at the side of the pool, fireworks suddenly erupted noisily into the air.

"Not yet!" screamed Mrs. Laggat-Brown furiously into the microphone.

Uneasy, Agatha looked across at the windows of the house and caught her breath. At one upstairs window, she saw the glint of what looked like a telescopic sight.

"Gun" she yelled. Spreading her arms wide and lunging forwards, she propelled Mrs. Laggat-Brown, Cassandra and Jason into the pool, falling in herself after them.

The fireworks had died away. Because of the noise of the fireworks, no one had heard Agatha's cry.

Mrs. Laggat-Brown was helped from the pool along with her daughter and then Jason.

Agatha swam to the steps and climbed out after them.

"There was a gun," she panted. "At that window. Up there!"

The two police officers ran into the house. Everyone waited. Cassandra began to cry.

At last the policeman and policewoman came out. "There's nothing there," said the police officer. "She must have imagined it."

"I didn't," protested Agatha, wiping water out of her eyes. "And who set off the fireworks?"

"Just go away," hissed Mrs. Laggat-Brown. "You have ruined my daughter's party. I will stop that cheque."

"Let me look upstairs," pleaded Agatha.

"What can you find that two officers of the law cannot? Go away, you horrible woman. GO!"

"I'm telling you, sir," said Police Constable Derry Carmichael later that evening to Detective Sergeant Bill Wong, "you should ha' been there."

He had just regaled Bill with a colourful account of how Agatha had pushed Mrs. Laggat-Brown, her daughter and Jason in the pool.

"Wait a minute," said Bill. "You say the fireworks went off before they should have? Why?"

"Oh, just a mistake, I reckon."

"You didn't ask?"

"Didn't reckon there was no need to. Them silly old women playing at detectives."

"Agatha Raisin is a friend of mine and she's no fool. When did the party break up?"

" 'Bout a half hour ago. Mrs. Laggat-Brown said it was all ruined and she didn't want to go on with it."

"I'm going round there. I was just about to go off duty, but it won't do any harm to take an extra look."

Mrs. Laggat-Brown, wrapped in a dressing-gown, gave Bill a lecture on the folly of women being able to set themselves up as detectives with no qualifications. Then, spurred on by Bill Wong's Asian features, she continued on with a diatribe against immigrant foreigners who were ruining the country.

Bill waited impassively until she had dried up and then said, "Nonetheless, I would like to search the upper rooms at the back of the house."

"But I have guests staying!"

"Is there a room up there which is not a guest-room?"

"Just a sort of box-room."

"I'll look there first. If you wouldn't mind . . ."

"Jason, would you be a dear? I am just too shocked to move."

"Come along," said Jason. "But the police have already looked."

When they reached the box-room, Jason looked on with amusement as Bill put a handkerchief over the handle before opening the door. Bill also switched on the light with the handkerchief and ordered Jason to wait outside.

The room was full of boxes labelled "Old Clothes," "Books," "China," piled on either side, leaving a passage to the window. The window was open at the bottom. Bill went slowly towards the window, peering at the floor. Then he knelt down. There was a dark stain on the uncarpeted boards near the window. He bent his nose down to the floor and sniffed. "Well, I'll be damned," he whispered. "I think that's gun oil."

He stood up and looked around while Jason waited impatiently outside. Bill took a pencil torch out of his pocket and began to shine it in the dark areas between the boxes. The thin beam of light picked out something shiny. Bill moved a box to one side and bent down again. An ejected cartridge shell.

He retreated out of the room. "No one has to be allowed in here until a forensic team arrives."

"What do you mean?" asked Jason.

"Mrs. Raisin was right and if it hadn't been for her prompt action, one of you would be dead."

Agatha and Emma sat in the office the following morning, wondering what to do. "I suppose I'd better send her cheque back," said Agatha, "or rather, since you cashed it, send her the money back."

Miss Simms looked up from painting her long nails. "Me, I think you saw something, Mrs. Raisin."

Emma was silently enjoying Agatha's distress. Agatha was usually always so confident about everything.

"What you got to smile about?" demanded Miss Simms sharply.

"I'm sorry," said Emma, flustered. "But if it wasn't that this will affect the business when it gets in the local papers, it would have been very funny, the way Agatha shoved them in the pool."

"It was too late for the local papers, thank God," said Agatha.

"I'm afraid someone is going to tell them," said Emma. "So many guests."

The phone rang, making them all jump.

"Raisin Detective Agency," fluted Miss Simms. Then she covered the receiver and hissed, "It's her. Mrs. Laggat-Brown."

"Tell her I'm dead," groaned Agatha. "No, on second thoughts, I may as well get it over with."

"Hello," said Agatha and then listened hard as Mrs. Laggat-Brown's voice quacked down the phone. "We'll be right over," said Agatha.

She put down the receiver and beamed in triumph. "I was right! Bill Wong, bless his cotton socks, went over there later and found gun oil and a spent cartridge. Come on, Emma, we're back in business. While we're out, Miss Simms, phone Douglas and Sammy and see if they've got anything on the Benington case."

Emma followed Agatha out feeling guilty. She had phoned the local paper late last night. It was just, she had thought at the time, that it was all for Agatha's good. She was so . . . well . . . rumbustious, she needed to be taken down a peg. She had given a false name. Emma comforted herself with the thought that the papers would call on Mrs. Laggat-Brown today and learn the truth.

There was a police mobile unit already set up in the grounds of the manor. Police were combing through the bushes. Agatha rang the bell and it was answered by Cassandra. "Mum's in the drawing-room with the police," she said. "You'd better go on in."

Detective Inspector Wilkes, Bill Wong and a woman constable were all in the drawing-room facing Mrs. Laggat-Brown and Jason.

Wilkes looked up as Agatha entered and said, "Ah, Mrs. Raisin, we were coming to see you when we'd finished our interviews here. Wait over there."

It appeared to be coming to the end of a long interview. Mrs. Laggat-Brown was protesting over and over again that she had no idea who should wish to stop the engagement. Cassandra did not have any jilted or jealous boyfriends and Jason had never known anyone dangerous or mad.

"Right," said Wilkes finally. "Mrs. Raisin, if you could just step outside to the mobile unit, we'll take your statement."

When Agatha had finished telling the police the little she knew, she returned to the house followed by Emma.

"You really must help me," pleaded Mrs. Laggat-Brown. "It's all so terrifying."

"Emma will sort out the details of our employment later," said Agatha. "Now, whoever got into the house must have known about that box-room. And who gave the order to start the fireworks?"

"Joe Gilchrist from the village had set them up. He said he heard a voice like mine shouting, 'Joe, start the fireworks now!'"

"So there was a female, an accomplice?"

"Seems like it." Mrs. Laggat-Brown twisted a handkerchief in her thin beringed fingers.

"I must ask you again about your husband," said Agatha. "Is there any reason he would try to stop Cassandra's engagement?"

"No, none at all. He couldn't have known about the party. I tried to get in touch with him, but his firm said he had taken a leave of absence."

"What is the name of his firm?"

"Chater's, in Lombard Street, in the City."

"Had he been there long?"

"Quite a number of years. But it can't be Jeremy. He adores Cassandra."

"When did you last hear from him?"

"It was on Cassandra's birthday, last May. He sent her a beautiful diamond bracelet."

"Did he never come to see her?"

"Not since the divorce."

"Which was when?"

"Three years ago."

"And you say it was an amicable divorce?"

"Oh, yes."

She's lying, thought Agatha suddenly. I don't know why but I feel she's lying.

Cassandra came bursting into the room. "Daddy's here!"

"What?"

"The police are talking to him. He's been abroad. He was just telling me about it when the police came up and took him to that caravan thing of theirs."

"He'll be so angry with me," whimpered Mrs. Laggat-Brown.

"Why?" asked Agatha.

"He'll think I haven't been looking after Cassandra properly."

"Now, how can he say that?" asked Agatha. "You were unable to get him after you received the threatening letter, weren't you?"

Mrs. Laggat-Brown looked down at her hands. The large rings on her fingers sent little prisms of light darting around the room. "No, I couldn't get him."

"This party must have been planned for a long time. Didn't he reply to the invitation?"

"Cassandra, dear," said her mother. "Could you get me a cup of coffee?"

She waited until her daughter had left the room and said, "I didn't send him an invitation."

"Why?"

"Oh, I don't know. I mean, he wanted the divorce, not me. I'm the one who has to take care of Cassandra. I didn't want him swanning up at the last minute and taking over. Mrs. Raisin, I do want to employ your services. Send me any forms to sign. At the moment, I would like to rest. I will talk to you later."

"Would you ask your husband to come and see me? Or call me when he's free?"

"I'll do that. Now, please leave me."

As the entrance to the manor was blocked by police cars, Agatha had parked out on the road. As she made her way out of the gate, a reporter from the local paper hailed her. "Agatha, what have you got to tell us?"

Agatha gave them a succinct account of her bravery and how she had saved Cassandra's life. She did not mention Emma. The photographer took Agatha's photo while the reporter said, "Funny, we thought at first there was nothing in it. Someone doesn't like you. Some woman phoned the paper last night to say you'd made an absolute fool of yourself. You've got an enemy."

"Did she leave a name?"

"No, anonymous tip-off."

"What kind of voice?"

"Posh."

"Probably one of the guests," murmured Emma.

Agatha had planned to go on as she had in the past, concentrating all her efforts on the attempted shooting of Cassandra. But small cases began to come into the detective agency and they had to be dealt with. Agatha was too good a business woman to run her detective agency into the red by dealing with only one case at a time.

There were requests to find missing teenagers, missing dogs and cats, or errant husbands and wives. At least Mr. Bennington was finally proved to be philandering and his grim wife took away the evidence with great satisfaction. To Agatha's relief, she did not demur over paying for the electronic surveillance.

Bill Wong, calling at the office one day, listened to Agatha's complaints and suggested she employ a retired police detective as well. He recommended a Patrick Mullen and gave Agatha the man's phone number.

"So," said Agatha, "what type of rifle was used? You've been able to find that out from the spent casing?"

"It's still in a queue at the forensics lab, Agatha. But we've interrogated the husband thoroughly."

"Great! And? He was supposed to come and see me, you know."

"He's got a cast-iron alibi. At the time of the shooting he was holidaying in Paris. Small hotel on the Boulevard Saint-Michel. Staff saw him that evening, as clear as day. He arrived back at the hotel at six o'clock and went out for a couple of hours, returned and went straight to bed. There is no way he could have nipped across the Channel and fired a gun at anyone. There is one lead, however."

"What's that?"

"Jason, the fiancé, seems squeaky-clean. But his father was once in prison for insider trading."

"But what's that got to do with killing Cassandra?"

"Turns out the couple have already made out their wills. If Cassandra dies, everything goes to Jason."

"Has she got anything? I mean, doesn't Mummy have all the money?"

"Last year, Cassandra won a million in the lottery."

"Blimey. So what does Jason's father have to say for himself?"

"That's the interesting thing. He was seen in the neighbourhood on the day of the party. Now he's disappeared."

"What about Jason's mother?"

"She divorced Harrison when he went to prison. No one seems to know where she's living. We've got a police guard on the house, but we can't keep guarding them indefinitely. We just don't have the resources. What with this government closing down country police stations one after the other, we've got an even bigger area to cover."

"I'll phone this detective you recommended," said Agatha. "Emma's been working hard, but I could do with an expert. Have you got a description of Jason's father?"

"Tall, thin, black-and-grey hair, large nose, black eyes, in his mid-fifties and evidently spry for his age. First name is Harrison. Like Harrison Ford. He hasn't worked since he got out of prison last year. Don't know where he's been living or what on."

"Maybe Cassandra has been giving him money."

"She denies that and I think she's telling the truth."

"I'd better pay the Laggat-Browns another call," said Agatha.

Firstly, after Bill had left, she phoned Patrick Mullen. He said he was interested in the job and would call round at the office in the early evening. Emma was out looking for a lost teenager, Sammy and Douglas were working on errant husbands and wives, so Agatha set out alone.

She planned to ask around Herris Cum Magna to see if there had been any other sightings of Jason's father, but first she went to the manor-house. Mrs. Laggat-Brown herself answered the door. "Oh, Mrs. Raisin," she fluted. "Do come in. Have you found anything?"

"Working hard on it," said Agatha, not wanting to admit that she had barely started. "Has your husband left? I thought he was coming to see you."

"Come into the drawing-room and I'll explain."

Agatha followed her through a shadowy hall and into a chintzy drawing-room that looked as if it had been furnished by Laura Ashley on an off-day.

"The fact is," said Mrs. Laggat-Brown, "that Jeremy and I have got together again. He's living here but commuting up to the City."

"And is Cassandra happy about this?"

"Of course. She adores her father."

"Where is she now?"

"Bermuda."

"Bermuda?"

"I decided to send her and Jason away on holiday for their safety."

"Mrs. Laggat-Brown . . ."

"Oh, do call me Catherine."

"Very well. I'm Agatha. Catherine, do the police know where Cassandra and Jason are?"

"Yes, the chief constable is a friend of mine and he thought it was a very good idea."

"I gather Jason's father was seen in the vicinity. You didn't tell me he had a criminal record."

Catherine flushed slightly. "Well, he's served his sentence and it's so much better to forget things like that, don't you think?"

"Not when you're dealing with attempted murder. Any more letters?"

"None at all."

"Did the police find any fingerprints on the letter or where the stationery had been bought?"

"No. I gather they've just finished their tests."

"No DNA from the flap?" asked Agatha, who was now thinking of all the questions she had failed to ask Bill.

"Self-sealing kind."

"Will Mr. Laggat-Brown be home this evening?"

"Yes, he comes home on the commuter train. Gets in at Moreton at six-thirty."

"Tell him to phone me." Agatha opened her handbag and extracted a card. "I would really like to talk to him. He might just remember something about someone."

"Very well. I'll try. You see, the fact is, he's rather angry with me for engaging you. He says it should be left to the police and all amateurs do is mess things up. The thing is, to keep him quiet, I told him I'd fired you."

Agatha looked at her curiously. "You don't seem to have enjoyed your freedom from marriage very much, Catherine. You're back with him and it seems he gives the orders."

"But one does so need a man around," sighed Catherine. "I mean, a woman feels so silly and alone without a man. The feminists say a woman needs a man like a fish needs a bicycle, but that always struck me as being rather stupid. I mean, why should they speak for fish? For all they know, fish might like a bicycle if they had the choice."

"I'll get back to you," said Agatha before Catherine could indulge in any more mad philosophy. "Is there a pub in the village?"

"The Oaks. Right in the centre. Turn left as you go out of the gate."

Agatha parked outside The Oaks. It was lunch-time and she was hungry. She hated to admit it, but she missed her usually lazy life.

She missed her cats and her talks with Mrs. Bloxby. She even missed the evenings with the ladies' society. She and Emma had been working every evening as well as every day. Agatha sighed as she pushed open the door of the pub. Thank God for Emma. She had turned out to be a good friend and a hard worker.

Emma went into the office and sat down and eased her long feet out of her shoes. "Rough day?" said Miss Simms.

"Too much walking in the heat," sighed Emma. "But I found that missing girl. I'll give you the notes to type up after lunch."

"I think I'll nip out and get something," said Miss Simms. She slid her long legs out from behind the desk. How can she go around in heels like that without her ankles swelling? wondered Emma. "Can I get you something?" asked Miss Simms.

"A ham sandwich, thank you."

"Brown or white?"

"Brown."

"Lettuce?"

"Yes, but no mayonnaise."

"Okey-dokey. See ya."

Emma massaged her feet. She looked forward to telling Agatha about her latest success. Agatha was so grateful. Emma felt guilty now about having given the newspaper that malicious call. Agatha deserved loyalty.

The door opened and a man breezed in. He was in his late forties and impeccably tailored. He had small neat features and fair hair.

"Aggie here?" he asked, looking around.

"No, Mrs. Raisin is out on a case."

"I'm Charles Fraith."

"Oh, you're the one who recommended us to Mrs. Laggat-Brown."

"That's me."

"I'm Emma Comfrey. I work with Agatha. I'm a detective."

Charles smiled. "You look a worn-out one. What about a spot of lunch?"

"I've just sent out for a sandwich."

"Forget it. Come on."

Over lunch, Charles listened while Emma told him all about the agency, rather stressing her successes and minimizing those of Agatha. Then she told this sympathetic listener the story of her life and bored Charles murmured, "How amazing," and, "Really!"

By the end of the lunch, Emma Comfrey was deeply in love with Sir Charles Fraith.

Agatha always marvelled that some of these tucked-away village pubs managed to survive. This one had a good few customers, and like most pubs these days, was set up with tables for eating.

She ordered fish and chips and when the waitress brought them asked her if a Mr. Harrison Peterson had been in the pub recently. "The police were asking that," said the buxom girl, leaning a hip against the table and ignoring the signalling hands of some of the other diners. "I tole them, he come in here two days, I think, afore the big party."

"Do you have rooms? I mean, does anyone know if he stayed in the village?"

"No, we don't let rooms, and besides, what with them big cars everyone's got, he could have come down from London."

"Jess!" shouted the landlord from behind the bar. "Customers!"

Jess moved away. Agatha ate her fish and chips and wondered what to do. The police would have conducted a door-to-door search. She decided to take a break and go home and see her cats and call on Mrs. Bloxby.

The cats looked singularly uninterested when she came in the door. Agatha sighed. Every time she left them alone for any length of time, the cats seemed to transfer their affections to her cleaner, Doris Simpson. The weather was still warm. She let the cats out into the garden. Then she closed the house up again and made her way along the dusty cobbled streets to the vicarage.

Agatha's hand hovered over the bell. The vicar always looked at her as if she were an unwelcome visitor. She walked round to the gate that led to the vicarage garden and saw Mrs. Bloxby dead-heading roses. Agatha noticed with a pang that her friend looked tired. Her gentle face had lines Agatha had not noticed before and her slim figure drooped.

She unlatched the gate and walked in. "Oh, Mrs. Raisin. How nice. Let me bring some tea out into the garden."

"Don't bother. I've just had lunch. You look tired."

"It's the heat. Come and sit down. The parish duties are heavier than usual. Quite a number of our old people are suffering from the heat. I was going to fund-raise to buy them all electric fans, but wouldn't you know it, the shops are all sold out. Really, one would think some entrepreneur would bring truckloads of them over from Taiwan or somewhere. I keep telling them to drink lots of water, but then, some of them have arthritis and it is so painful to go to the loo that they cut down on fluids."

"Don't they have carers?"

"Yes, they do, and district nurses and Meals on Wheels, but a lot of them are frightened of death and Alf is overworked as it is. So I have to help. You do see that."

"Yes," said Agatha, although she privately thought she might well have left them all to the care of the state if their roles had been reversed.

"Tell me about the latest case, Mrs. Raisin."

Agatha settled back in her chair and began to talk. As she talked, Mrs. Bloxby's eyelids fluttered and then closed. Agatha lowered her voice. Soon Mrs. Bloxby was fast asleep. Agatha sat enjoying the peace of the old garden and the next thing she knew Mrs. Bloxby was shaking her arm. "Do wake up, Mrs. Raisin. We both fell asleep and I was frightened you might be missing appointments."

Agatha looked at her watch. "Good heavens. I'd better go. I've got a retired detective to see!"

Patrick Mullen was a tall, cadaverous man who rarely smiled. Agatha discussed wages with him and then told Miss Simms to show him the files on the various unsolved cases.

"What about that shooting business?" he asked.

"I'll put you on it if we get some of this backlog cleared up," said Agatha. "Now I've got to run. There's someone arriving at Moreton-in-Marsh I've got to see."

The train, as usual, was late. Agatha waited beside the flower-beds on Moreton station and wished she had asked for a description of Mr. Laggat-Brown. This detective business was difficult. So many questions one forgot to ask.

At last she could see the train down at the end of the long, long stretch of line. He would probably be travelling first-class.

That would mean the carriages at the back if it was a Great Western train or the one cramped little bit of carriage for first-class passengers if it should turn out to be a Thames train.

What would he look like? She conjured up a picture of a small fussy man with thinning hair in a business suit.

The train drew in and the passengers poured off. A lot of people were now commuting between London and the country. A man who looked like her mental image came bustling up. "Mr. Laggat-Brown?" asked Agatha.

He stared at her and then walked past. "Were you looking for me?" asked a voice.

Agatha found herself staring up at an extremely handsome man. "Mr. Laggat-Brown?"

"That's me. Who are you?"

"Agatha Raisin."

"Oh, that detective female."

"Can we talk?"

"If you must. But I told my wife that to go to the expense of paying a detective agency when the police are doing all they can is ridiculous. Still, it's her business. Let's sit on that bench over there."

Agatha was suddenly conscious of her crumpled linen suit and flat heels. Jeremy Laggat-Brown was tall with a square-cut tanned face and bright blue eyes. His thick hair was slightly curled and pure white. His suit was a miracle of good tailoring.

"Now, what can I do for you?" he asked. He lit a cigarette and Agatha opened her handbag and took out her own cigarette case. Cigarette cases had come back into fashion because of all the nasty government warnings on the packets.

"I wondered, of course, if you had any idea of why anyone would want to shoot your daughter?"

"None in the slightest. Must be some maniac."

"Do you think it could be Jason's father?"

"I don't. I mean, what would he gain by it? He was in prison for fraud, not psychopathic killing." He suddenly smiled at her. "I must say, you're not what I expected from my wife's description."

"And what was that?"

"Never mind. I didn't expect an attractive woman."

Somewhere deep in Agatha's treacherous stomach rumbled that old sexual buzz.

"Jason would inherit if Cassandra were killed."

"And you mean the father would hope to get money from the son? Far-fetched. One does not think of a young daughter as dying. The whole thing's weird. You know what I really think? I think there's some mad sharpshooter in the neighbourhood who decided to use us for target practice."

"And what about the threatening letter?"

"Same nutter, I suppose. Lots of class jealousy around."

"You haven't always lived at the manor, have you?"

"The manor-house belonged to the Felliet family for centuries, but they went broke and we bought it. The villagers went on as if the queen had been dethroned."

"When did you buy the manor?"

"Only about eight years ago."

"And where are the Felliets now?"

"That'll be Sir George and his lady. Don't really know."

"And you are reconciled with your wife?"

"Well, in a way. We won't be remarrying or anything like that. We rub along all right. Doing it to please Cassandra."

"And you were in Paris at the time of the shooting?"

He grinned. "And plenty of witnesses to that fact. Tell you what, time's getting on and I promised Catherine I'd be home for dinner. Why don't you and I have a meal later in the week and then I really will have time to answer all your questions?"

"I would like that." Agatha tried not to sound too eager. "I'll give you my card."

When he left, Agatha decided to go home and spend a quiet evening repairing her face and tinting the roots of her hair. She had thick brown hair but grey was beginning to show through.

Would he really phone? It wasn't as if he was married. What should she wear?

She could hear faintly the warning voice of Mrs. Bloxby. "You are addicted to falling in love." But Agatha's mind blotted it out. It was so wonderful to have a man to dream about, the colourful dreams filling up that empty hole that had been in her head for so long. Without dreams, Agatha was left with Agatha, a person she did not like very much, although that was something she would never admit to herself.

Agatha fed her cats, microwaved herself a shepherd's pie and then microwaved some chips to go with it. Then she went upstairs for a long soak in the bathtub before tackling her hair. It would be better, she thought, to have a hairdresser do the tinting, so she compromised by using a "brunette" shampoo, colour guaranteed to last through three washes.

She studied her face closely in the "fright" mirror, one of those magnifying ones, and seizing the tweezers, plucked two hairs from her upper lip.

Agatha was just wrapping herself in her dressing-gown when

she heard someone moving about downstairs. She looked around for a weapon and then picked up a can of hair lacquer to spray in the intruder's eyes. It was only when she reached the bottom of the stairs that she realized she could have phoned the police from the extension in the bedroom.

The bottom stair creaked beneath her feet.

"That you, Aggie?" called a lazy voice from the sitting-room. Charles Fraith.

"You might have knocked!" raged Agatha. "You gave me a fright."

"And you gave me the keys, remember?"

"No, I don't. I'd forgotten you still had them."

"I must say, you do look a picture, Aggie."

Agatha realized her face was covered in cream and her hair wrapped up in a towel. She made to retreat and then shrugged. "You'll just need to put up with it, Charles. Drink?"

Emma watched hungrily from the side window. She had seen Charles drive up. She waited and waited for him to leave. He couldn't surely be staying the night, could he?

At last, tiredness drove her off to bed. Emma resolved to call on Mrs. Bloxby in the morning. Agatha would assume she was out on one of the cases when she didn't turn up at the office. Mrs. Bloxby would know what was going on.

Mrs. Bloxby wondered why Emma had called. She served her coffee while Emma chatted aimlessly about the weather. At last Mrs. Bloxby said, "Aren't you due at work?"

"I don't go into the office much," said Emma. "So many little cases to work on."

Mrs. Bloxby let a long silence form between them, hoping Emma would take the hint and go.

"Sir Charles Fraith stayed at Agatha's last night," said Emma, breaking the silence.

"Oh, he's back, is he? They're old friends."

Emma let out a false giggle. "Just friends, I suppose?"

"Yes."

"All the same," said Emma, putting her cup down on the saucer with a clatter, "Agatha doesn't seem to care much for her reputation, having a man to stay overnight."

"A lot of the villagers have friends to stay overnight," said Mrs. Bloxby, looking curiously at Emma's flushed face, "and nobody thinks anything of it."

"Charles is a very attractive man. He took me to lunch yesterday."

"And Mrs. Raisin is a very attractive woman. But I assure you, nobody is gossiping about her relation with Sir Charles."

"Agatha, attractive?"

"I believe men find her sexy. Now, I hate to rush you, but I have parish duties to attend to."

"Of course. I'll be on my way."

Oh dear, thought Mrs. Bloxby. I do believe poor Mrs. Comfrey has fallen in love. Isn't it odd, all those women's magazines going on about sex the whole time and they never seem to realize that there's a silent majority of women who crave romance and find talk about the tricks of the brothel and vibrators and so on disgusting and humiliating. No warnings against romantic obsession, and the later in life it hits, the more dangerous.

Mrs. Bloxby placed a straw had on her head and set out to

make parish calls. She never even considered warning Agatha simply because she received so many confidences that she had trained herself over the years to forget them immediately. The idea that remaining silent might put Agatha's life in danger never crossed her mind.

FOUR

†

"WHO does this Jeremy Laggat-Brown work for?" asked Charles over breakfast.

"Think it was something like Chater's."

"Good firm. Lombard Street. I know someone there. I'll give them a ring."

When Charles went to the phone, Agatha sipped her coffee and smoked a cigarette, wishing it were like the old days when she hadn't set up as a professional detective and had only the one case to bother about.

Charles came back, grinning. "Now here's a thing. Laggat-Brown isn't with them any more. He's set up his own business—import/export."

"Importing and exporting what?"

"Electronic bits and pieces. Got an office up a dingy stair in

Fetter Lane, according to my old school pal. Our Jeremy travels a lot. Seems to be a one-man operation, with a secretary to look after things when he's not there."

"Why did he leave Chater's?"

"Evidently said he was tired of stockbroking."

"No leaving under a cloud, anything like that?"

"I'll push further."

"I should really put you on the books," began Agatha, then added hurriedly as she saw a mercenary gleam in Charles's eyes, "but I'm overstretched as it is."

He sighed. "To think Cassandra won the lottery. Doesn't seem fair. Only poor people should win the lottery."

"Like you?"

"Like me."

"Charles, one of your suits would feed a family for a year."

"Which reminds me, I haven't paid my tailor's bill. You said something about the Felliets who used to own the manor. I know George. Was at school with him. Why are you interested in the Felliets?"

"I thought they might be able to tell us more about the Laggat-Browns than the Laggat-Browns have been telling me. Do you know where they live?"

"Let me think. I know. Ancombe. They'll be in the phone book. By the way, I took your assistant, Emma, out for lunch yesterday."

"Did you? That's nice. Should we go and visit the Felliets?"

"All right. Like old times. What about the detective agency?"

"They don't need me at the moment. Runs itself. Emma and a retired detective I've hired can deal with everything."

*   *   *

The Felliets turned out to live in a small cottage on the outskirts of Ancombe. Even small cottages in the Cotswolds now cost quite a lot of money, but as Charles held open the garden gate for her, Agatha reflected that it must have been a sore climb-down for the Felliets to have to give up their manor-house for this.

A small rotund man in his mid-forties wearing stone-washed jeans and an open-necked striped shirt answered the door. "Why, Charles," he exclaimed, "what brings you here? Haven't seen you in yonks. Come in."

They followed him into a little living-room. Agatha glanced around. It was as if a country-house drawing-room had been scaled right down. There were pretty pieces of antique furniture, and family portraits crowded the walls.

"My wife's out," said George Felliet, "but I've got a pot of coffee in the kitchen. That do?"

"Fine," said Charles. "Agatha, George. George, Agatha."

"We don't have a sit-in kitchen," said George. "Wait there and I'll fetch the coffee."

"His old man was a bit of a gambler," said Charles while they waited. "Then the death duties took a lot of what they had."

"Is he a baronet like you?"

"Yes, very old family. The manor-house had been in the family for centuries."

"Pity."

George came in bearing a tray. "Here we go. Milk, Agatha?"

"Black will do."

"Charles, help yourself. Now, what brings you?"

"Agatha is a detective," said Charles, "and she's investigating that shooting at the manor. Have you any idea why someone would want to shoot their daughter?"

"No. Had it been the Laggat-Brown woman, I could have understood it. Did you see what she did to the manor? No soul. The name isn't really Laggat-Brown."

"Oh, what is it?"

"Ryan. For some reason Jeremy Ryan decided that Laggat-Brown sounded better and changed it by deed poll."

"You'd think he'd have chosen something grander," said Charles.

"I tell you, that lot have only a veneer of sophistication. Underneath, they're as common as muck. She made her money out of Daddy's business. And do you know what that was?"

"No."

"Dog biscuits."

"You're being snobbish, George. Nothing up with dog biscuits."

George sighed. His rubicund face and small mouth gave him the look of a hurt baby.

"I am, I know. It was just the way she went on. Rubbing salt in the wound. Kept saying things like, 'If you can't afford to keep up a place like this, it's much more sensible to sell it to someone like me who can.' Dealt with us with a mixture of pity and contempt. I really hate that woman. And if I really hate that woman, then, believe me, she's rubbed someone else up the wrong way."

"Where's the wife?" asked Charles.

"Down in the village, shopping."

"And Felicity?"

"She's abroad. Travels a lot."

"What does she do at the moment?"

"Assistant in some dress shop."

"Which dress shop?"

"Charles, I'm getting angry about all these questions. One would think you suspected the Felliet family of having tried to kill that lumpy daughter of hers."

"I'm sorry, George," said Charles. "I'm so used to going around with Agatha trying to find out who murdered whom that I get a bit carried away. Let's talk about other things."

Agatha drank her coffee and listened to their reminiscences and longed for a cigarette, but could see no sign of an ashtray anywhere.

At last Charles decided to leave. As they drove off, he said, "Poor old George. I really did rile him up with all those questions. It can't be anything to do with them. I wish we had the powers of the police. Maybe it would be easier for us to find Peterson then. You know, Agatha, you said you'd engaged that retired detective. Retired detectives usually keep up their contacts in the police. Might be better to let him take over for a bit."

Agatha grinned ruefully. "And leave me with all the lost cats, dogs and children? Still, it might be worth a try."

Charles accompanied her to the office. Patrick Mullen was dictating notes to Miss Simms, who was typing them out on her computer with such long nails that Agatha wondered how she managed.

Emma was sitting on the sofa with a small Yorkshire terrier at her feet. "I've phoned the owner," said Emma. "She's coming round."

She did not look at Charles, who said breezily, "Hi, Emma!"

Emma murmured something and bent down to stroke the dog.

"Patrick," said Agatha, "stop what you're doing. I need you on this shooting case."

The owner of the dog came in as Agatha was talking and was effusive in her thanks.

When she had left, Emma consulted her notes. Another missing teenager, seventeen-year-old girl called Kimberly Bright. Emma sighed. Charles came and sat beside her. "You look fed up. What's up?"

"I've got to start looking for a missing seventeen-year-old. It's difficult for me because there's such a generation gap, I don't know anything about how they behave these days."

"Miss Simms would know," said Charles. He interrupted Agatha. "Agatha, Emma's got a seventeen-year-old to look for. Miss Simms might have a better idea about how to go about it. Why don't you let her have a go and Emma can do the typing?"

"Ooh, I'd love to try," said Miss Simms.

"Oh, all right," said Agatha. "Give Miss Simms the file, Emma. I'm taking Patrick out for an early lunch so I can continue filling him in on all the details."

Charles raised his eyebrows. He reflected that Agatha, preoccupied as she now was, could be amazingly rude and insensitive.

"I'm sure Emma could do with a break as well," he said. "I'll take you to lunch, Emma."

Emma flushed up with pleasure. But her face fell when Agatha snapped, "And who's going to answer the phones?"

"I'll stay here," said Miss Simms. "It'll give me a chance to study the photographs and read up on where you've looked, Emma."

Emma was momentarily diverted by the thought that it was ridiculous that a young woman like Miss Simms should call her by her first name and yet she herself was somehow bound by the ladies' society tradition of second names only.

Then, to her dismay, Agatha turned in the doorway and said, "Sorry, Charles, I should have asked you as well."

"Yes, you should. But I've asked Emma to lunch, so run along."

So Emma was in seventh heaven. Excited as a schoolgirl, she chattered about her life all through lunch, saying that her husband had bullied her and that her colleagues had bullied her. She was sure that she was bringing out the strong protective side of Charles's character, not knowing that he didn't have one and was damning her as a professional victim.

"This Jeremy Laggat-Brown who used to be Ryan," said Patrick over lunch. "His Paris alibi checks out?"

"Watertight. And why should he want to shoot his own daughter?"

"Well, I'll start in Herris Cum Magna and then I'll speak to Jason Peterson this evening," said Patrick.

"You can't. He's in Bermuda, remember?"

"Forgot. I've still got contacts in the police. Before you asked me, I decided to do a bit of checking up on my own. I'll find out from them what they're doing about tracing Harrison Peterson. They'll have the airports and ports covered, I know that, but I don't want to go over old ground locally. Also, I'll check the libraries for old reports about his fraud case and get a photograph."

"Have the police found out yet what kind of gun was used?"

"Didn't I tell you? Now, that's a very interesting thing. It was a sniper rifle. A Parker-Hale M-85. It's a first-rate sniper rifle, capable of precision fire up to ranges of nine hundred metres. The weapon has a silent safety catch, a threaded muzzle for flash suppressor, and an integral dovetail mount that accepts a variety of sights. Sort of thing a professional assassin would use."

"I don't think a professional assassin would bother to send a threatening letter first," Agatha pointed out.

"True. This rifle is made by Sable Defence Industries here in the UK. Police are going through the books there, trying to trace all the rifles that have been sold."

"Have forensics found out anything else?"

"Only that we're dealing with one very cool customer. He wore gloves and swept his way out of the box-room so there would be no fingerprints. The corridor and stairs are thickly carpeted."

"He didn't need to leave in a rush," said Agatha bitterly. "I mean, the police went into the house, but I don't think they even went in to the box-room. Just pushed the door open and looked. Well, good hunting. To tell you the truth, I'm not enjoying this detective agency business much. I hate the missing teenager ones because the parents are naturally distraught and it's awfully hard trying to find someone the police were unable to."

"The whole police force will search far and wide for a missing child," said Patrick, "but once they reach the late teens, the search isn't so urgent. What are Sam and Douglas doing?"

"Adultery cases. They pay well."

"I'll get off to Herris Cum Magna."

"Wait a minute. Harrison Peterson was seen on the day of the party in Herris Cum Magna. Who saw him?"

"I got a tip-off. A Mrs. Blandford. I'll start with her."

Agatha made her way back to the office. Patrick had made her feel like an amateur. Why hadn't she tried to get Bill to tell her the name of the person who had spotted Harrison?

To her annoyance, the office was locked. She unlocked the door and walked in. Emma had left a note. "Not feeling very well. Had to go home and lie down. Miss Simms is out on that job. Emma."

The afternoon dragged on. Miss Simms did not return and there was no sign of Charles. At last Agatha locked up and went home, calling first at Emma's cottage, but there was no reply.

She went into her own cottage, calling, "Charles!" The house was silent. She went upstairs to the spare bedroom. Charles had arrived with an overnight bag. It was gone. Agatha realized she had offended him and knew from experience that an offended Charles could stay away for quite a long time.

She went downstairs again just as the phone started to ring. It was Roy Silver, her one-time assistant, on the other end of the line.

"Aggie!" he cried. "I haven't heard from you in ages. Feel like doing some free-lance PR?"

"I can't, Roy. I've started up my own detective agency."

"How exciting. Can I come down this weekend for a visit?"

"Of course. Are you driving down or taking the train?"

"The train. We're coming into the wrong-kind-of-the-leaves-on-the-line season and the trains will probably run late. I'll be down Friday about eight o'clock."

"Fine."

Agatha brightened up at the prospect of seeing Roy again, but she missed Charles. She went through to her desk with some computer disks which had the detective agency's accounts logged on them, put the disks in and began to go through the figures.

She noticed that she was beginning to actually show a small profit despite all the staff she had employed. The adultery cases were paying well and they were beginning to get quite a few from divorce lawyers.

She closed down the computer and was just about to phone Charles when her phone rang.

"Jeremy Laggat-Brown," said the voice at the other end. "Remember me?"

"Of course."

"Have you had dinner yet?"

"No, not yet."

"How about coming out to have a bite to eat with me?"

"That would be nice," said Agatha cautiously. "Will your wife be there?"

"Catherine's got a Women's Institute meeting tonight."

"Well, in that case . . ."

"Pick you up at eight? Where are you?" Agatha had put her home phone number along with the office number on her card but not her home address. She gave him directions. Then, when she replaced the receiver and looked at the clock, she let out a squawk. It was half past seven.

She fled up the stairs and began to tear clothes out of her wardrobe and place them on the bed. Then she decided she was wasting valuable time wondering what to wear when she should be making up her face.

Agatha at last descended the stairs just as the doorbell rang wearing a black sheath dress and very high heels and carrying a cashmere stole.

She opened the door and noticed with a sinking heart that Jeremy was dressed in jeans and an open-necked shirt.

"You look grand," he said.

"Maybe too grand. Should I change into something casual?"

"No, you're fine as you are."

Remember, Agatha cautioned herself, as she eased herself into his Mercedes, he may not be married but he's living with his ex-wife and she thinks they're getting together again.

He took her to a newly opened French restaurant in Broadway. "Shall I order for us?" he asked.

"Please," said Agatha on her best behaviour, although she privately thought he might at least have suggested she look at the menu.

When he had placed the order, he smiled at her with those deep blue eyes. James has blue eyes, thought Agatha, a sharp memory of her husband invading her brain. "Tell me about yourself and how you got into the detective business," he asked.

He was a good listener and Agatha loved to talk about herself and her adventures and so it was lucky for him that she did not really notice much what she was eating, although she did register that the confit de canard seemed to consist of rubbery pieces of near-raw duck in a sort of watery jam.

Over brandy and coffee, Agatha suddenly realized just how much she had been monopolizing the evening's conversation.

"You haven't told me a bit about yourself," she said guiltily. "How did you get into the import/export business?"

Was it her imagination, or did those eyes go hard for a moment? Then he smiled. "You *have* been doing your work. I got fed up stockbroking. I originally trained as an electronics engineer. I knew several of the top firms and so it was easy to start importing and exporting electronics. But surely this is all very boring. Have you found Harrison Peterson?"

"One of my staff, a retired police detective, is out looking for him. I suppose he must be the guilty party. Did you know him?"

"Only slightly when I was a stockbroker myself. I don't know that I approve of Cassandra's engagement to Jason. There's bad blood in that family."

"Do you think that Jason might have been in with his father in a plot to kill Cassandra?"

"Why should he?"

"They've made joint wills, Cassandra and Jason. And you know that Cassandra won the lottery. I hope that's not the case because the pair of them are together in Bermuda."

"Seems silly. Makes Jason or his father the obvious suspect. Jason is devoted to his father by all accounts."

"Where's the mother? Whoever tried to shoot Cassandra had a female accomplice."

"Jason never forgave her for divorcing his father. I don't know where she's living."

Agatha sighed. "You see? So many questions I forgot to ask. The police have probably found her."

Jeremy called for the bill and Agatha excused herself and went to the ladies' room. As she repaired her make-up, she began to fret. Will he ask me out again? Why on earth did I talk so much?

"Oh, grow up, Agatha!" she snarled at her reflection in the mirror. "He may not be married but he's as good as."

She went out. He rose to his feet. "I've enjoyed the evening immensely. We must do this again."

After a short pause in which Agatha had just been about to demand, "When?" and thought better of it, she said instead, "I should enjoy that very much."

He drove her home. She invited him in for a drink, but he replied that he should be getting home. Agatha went into her cottage feeling rather flat.

She checked her phone for messages and found there was one. It was from Patrick Mullen. "I've tracked Harrison Peterson. He's staying at a small pub that lets rooms called The Hereford in Evesham. We're meeting him tomorrow at ten. He says he's got a lot to tell us. I tried to get him to talk this evening. I didn't see him. He talked through the door. Should I go to the police with this?"

Agatha quickly phoned Patrick. "Don't go to the police," she ordered. "This is our coup. I'll see you in the office at nine."

Her evening with Jeremy was quickly forgotten. Agatha could barely sleep that night for excitement.

In the office the following morning, Agatha was only momentarily diverted by Emma's appearance. Emma's hair was now dyed blonde and she was skilfully made up. She was wearing a black trouser-suit of expensive cut. Agatha briefly reflected that Emma now looked like one of those well-preserved, ginny, big-toothed women one occasionally saw at game fairs. Agatha forgot that Emma had claimed to be ill.

"So, Patrick," she said, "how on earth did you get on to him?"

"I saw this Mrs. Blandford, a widow who lives in Herris Cum Magna. She knew him slightly. She gave him a cup of tea. She said he was sore at being left out of the engagement party. I said that was because his son didn't know where he was and she said that Harrison had told her that his son had been in touch with him but had said that Mrs. Laggat-Brown had refused to invite Harrison."

"The old cow. She never told me that."

"I asked where Harrison was now and she got all shifty and said if she'd known that, she'd have told the police. I picked up that she'd a soft spot for Harrison. At last she said he'd said something about having a room in a pub in Evesham. I checked out the pubs that let rooms—very few of them—armed with a description and traced him to The Hereford."

"Well done," said Agatha. "Let's get along there."

As they drove towards Evesham, Patrick said uneasily, "I've got a bad feeling about this. I feel we should have turned the whole thing over to the police."

"Patrick, Mrs. Laggat-Brown is paying heavily for my services. If the police get to him first, she may give them all the credit and cut back on my fee and I'm just beginning to show a profit."

"I know, I know. Just got a bad feeling in my water."

The Hereford was situated near Evesham railway station. Patrick parked in the car-park. "The pub'll still be closed," said Agatha.

"It's all right. You get to his room up a side staircase."

"No security," commented Agatha as Patrick opened the side door. "Anyone could walk in."

"Well, they're hardly expecting burglars in a dingy pub in Evesham. His room is number two."

They mounted the uncarpeted staircase which smelt of stale beer. Patrick knocked on the door. "Harrison? It's me. Patrick Mullen. Open up."

There was no reply.

"Damn," said Patrick. "Maybe he's flown. I should have told the police last night, Agatha."

"Try the door," urged Agatha.

He turned the handle and the door swung open. It was a small dark room furnished only with a wardrobe, a wash-basin, a table and chair and narrow bed.

And on that bed lay a man, face-down.

FIVE

†

"WAIT!" ordered Patrick as Agatha would have rushed forwards. He drew out two pairs of thin plastic gloves. "Put these on."

Agatha did as she was told, whispering, "He's not dead, is he?"

Patrick went to the figure on the bed and felt the neck. Then he straightened up. "There's no pulse."

They looked around. An empty bottle of sleeping pills and an empty bottle of vodka stood beside the bed. Against the vodka bottle was propped a folded sheet of paper. Patrick picked it up and opened it carefully.

"What does it say?" asked Agatha.

Patrick read: "I tried to kill Cassandra because I wanted Jason to get her money and give some to me so I could start my own business. Now I can't live with myself. I threw the rifle in the river."

"Typewritten?" asked Agatha.

"There's his computer and printer on the table. Blast. We've got to get out of here. If we go to the police now, they'll charge us with tampering with an investigation and I promised the Blandford woman I wouldn't get her into trouble."

"What about security cameras outside?"

"None. I checked. Come on. Let's go."

Once they were in the car and heading out of Evesham, Agatha said, "Anyone could have written that note."

"Nice thought," said Patrick, "but I've found that real-life cases are not like detective stories. If he said he did it, he did it. Don't tell anyone in the office about this."

"They were all listening when we were discussing going along."

Patrick stopped in a lay-by with a phone-box. "I'd better give the police an anonymous call and then get the hell back on the road because they can trace calls immediately they're made these days."

Agatha waited while Patrick went into the phone-box. He spoke briefly and then jumped back in the car. "Off we go," he said, "and as fast as possible. Now when we get to the office, we tell a white lie and say he's dead and the police got there before us, so we turned about."

"They're all very loyal. We could swear them to secrecy."

"I don't trust anybody."

"Okay, we'll do it your way. Means the end of working for Mrs. Laggat-Brown."

He shrugged. "Who needs her anyway? Cases are coming in by the day."

Agatha suddenly missed Charles. She felt uneasy about

Harrison's death. She felt she could think more clearly if she discussed it with Charles. Still, Roy was coming and he was always a good listener.

Mrs. Laggat-Brown phoned later that day to tell Agatha that Harrison had been found and that it was all such a relief. She ended by saying, "I should have followed Jeremy's advice and left the whole thing to the police and saved myself a lot of money."

Agatha longed to say that if it hadn't been for her agency's investigation, the case might never have been solved.

She phoned Charles, but his aunt said he had gone abroad.

Agatha sat and drummed her fingers on the desk. Then her eyes lit up. If by any chance it should turn out that there weren't any fingerprints on the vodka bottle or on the glass, then that would mean someone had faked the suicide.

She phoned Patrick on his mobile. "I'll check it out, Agatha," he said. "But I'm afraid you're going to have to get back to dogs, cats, divorces and missing teenagers."

Miss Simms entered, flushed with success, having not only found the missing teenager she had been looking for but having delivered the girl back to her parents.

"Oh, well done," said Agatha. "Let me build up a little more profit and I'll get another girl to do the secretarial work and put you on the road."

"You look lovely, Emma," said Miss Simms brightly. "What have you been doing to yourself? Got yourself a fella?"

Emma blushed. "Just felt like smartening up," she mumbled.

On Friday evening, Agatha picked up Roy from the station at Moreton-in-Marsh.

The young man was all in white—white raw-silk suit, white panama hat and white high-heeled boots.

"Now what are you supposed to be?" asked Agatha. "You look like the man from Del Monte."

"It's the cool look, sweetie," said Roy. "It's the ice cream look. This weather's been so hot. I assure you, I'm the new black."

"Do you want to eat out or in?"

"Out," said Roy, who had sampled Agatha's microwave cooking several times.

"What do you feel like eating?"

"Chinese."

"There a great one in Evesham. That's if you don't mind driving. I'm tired. It's been a gruelling week."

Between mouthfuls, as they picked their way with chop-sticks through a large Chinese meal, Agatha told him all about the Laggat-Brown case and the suicide of Harrison Peterson.

Her story took her right through the meal until the pot of green tea was being served.

"Well," said Roy, leaning back and patting fussily at his mouth with his napkin, "it all seems odd. I mean, he makes an appointment with this detective of yours and then kills himself."

"That's what I thought. But Patrick has contacts in the police and if there had been anything fishy, he'd let me know. I mean, Peterson typed the suicide note on his computer and printed it off. If anyone else had typed it for him, they'd have wiped the keys clean."

"I watch all these forensic detectives stories on television," said Roy. "The things they can find out."

"I don't think it actually works like that here," said Agatha.

"I mean, the labs are backed up with cases. They aren't going to look too hard when they've got a suicide note, an empty vodka bottle and an empty bottle of sleeping pills."

"Who supplied the sleeping pills? The doctor's name would be on the bottle."

"Why should I bother?"

"It would be interesting to know a bit about Harrison."

"I didn't think to look. I was so shocked. Maybe Patrick noticed."

Agatha rang Patrick's mobile and asked him. "You didn't notice either," Roy heard her say. "Any way of finding out? I know it seems odd but I'd just like to know. All right, thanks. I'll see you in the office on Monday."

"Don't you work weekends?" asked Roy when she had rung off.

"Usually. But I told everyone to have a rest. We've all been working long hours."

Emma watched from the side window of her cottage as Agatha and Roy drove up. She saw Roy lift a travel bag out of the boot and then follow Agatha indoors. To Emma's old-fashioned mind, a man stayed overnight with a woman for only one reason. It was disgusting. He was obviously years younger than Agatha. She wondered if dear Charles knew of this liaison.

She went back downstairs and looked at the details she had copied out of the *Peerage and Baronetage*. Charles owned Barfield House in Warwickshire. Her heart began to thump as she envisaged a plan. He had taken her for lunch twice. They were friends. She had heard Agatha trying to contact him but did not know Agatha had been told he was abroad. In the morning, she could drive out to his home and say she was working on a case in the neighbourhood. No harm in that. No harm at all.

The nights had turned blessedly cool, but the morning mists dispersed rapidly. Saturday promised to be yet another scorching day as Emma motored along the Fosseway into Warwickshire, her hands damp on the steering wheel with nerves, an ordnance survey map on the passenger seat beside her.

She turned off the Fosseway and down long narrow country lanes, searching for Barfield House. She nearly missed the entrance because there was not the name of the house on the gateposts but a sign saying "Private." Emma drove a long way up a wooded, twisting drive. Perhaps she would have turned back if the road had not been too narrow to make a turn. Then she was out of the woods and the road ran through fields. She drew onto a grassy verge as a tractor approached. The tractor stopped alongside her and the driver asked, "What are you doing here? This is private property."

"I am a friend of Sir Charles Fraith," said Emma crossly. He nodded and touched his cap and drove on.

Emma headed onwards, round a stable block, and there, suddenly, was the house.

In her dreams and fantasies about Charles—and they were many—Emma had imagined a Georgian mansion with a pillared portico. Barfield House was one of those Victorian mistakes. It was not even Victorian Gothic but built in the fake medieval style beloved by the Pre-Raphaelites. It was a large building with mullioned windows which sparkled in the sunlight.

"Here goes," muttered Emma.

She rang the bell set into the stone wall beside an enormous studded door.

A faded elderly lady answered the door, "Yes?" she asked, her pale grey eyes raking up and down Emma's long figure.

"I am here to see Charles."

"What's your name?"

"Emma Comfrey."

"And he was expecting you? He's gone abroad."

"No, but we're friends and I happened to be working in the neighbourhood and—"

"Not collecting for something, are you?"

"NO!"

"Who is it?" she heard Charles calling.

"Wait!" commanded the woman.

Emma waited. The woman retreated into the house and left the door open. Emma heard her calling, "Charles! Where are you? I've got some creature on the doorstep asking for you."

Emma, all newly blonded hair and new sky-blue linen suit, felt herself shrinking.

It was no use. She couldn't go through with it. She turned away towards her car.

"Do you want to see me?" called Charles's voice from the doorway.

Emma reluctantly turned.

"Good heavens! It's Emma, isn't it? And looking glamorous," said Charles gallantly.

He was wearing a striped dressing-gown over a pair of blue silk pyjamas. His feet were bare. Emma stared at his feet as if mesmerized.

"Now you're here, come in," said Charles. "Have some coffee."

"That woman called me a creature," said Emma, still looking at his feet.

"That woman is my aunt and she calls everyone a creature."

Mollified, Emma followed him in through a dark stone-flagged hall decorated with a few oil paintings badly in need of cleaning and a moth-eaten moose head.

"Gustav!" shouted Charles. "Coffee! In the study."

"Can't you get it?" came the reply. "I'm cleaning the silver."

"Coffee for two. Now!"

The study was as dark as the hall and lined from floor to ceiling with books. There were two comfortable armchairs with side tables by the fire. Charles lit a lamp and opened a window.

"Sit down, Emma," said Charles. "Does Agatha know you're here?"

"It's silly of me but I was working nearby looking for a missing teenager and I suddenly decided to call on impulse. Do forgive me. I should have phoned first."

"That would have been a good idea. Still, you're here. How's the shooting case going?"

"Oh, haven't you seen the paper yet?"

"No, what's been going on? Ah, Gustav. How do you take your coffee, Emma?"

"Two sugars and no milk, please."

Gustav had grizzled hair, small black eyes and a long mobile mouth. He was dressed in black trousers and a white shirt open at the neck.

He deftly poured coffee for both of them.

His black eyes studied Emma for a long moment. Then he turned to Charles. "You really ought to be locked up," he said.

"Bugger off, Gustav," said Charles amiably.

"Who was that?" asked Emma.

"My butler. Of course no one, least of all me, can afford a full-time butler these days, so Gustav is a maid of all work."

"He should show more respect."

"Did you come to criticize the staff?" Charles's normally pleasant voice had an edge to it.

Emma's hand holding the cup shook. "I'm so sorry," she babbled.

"Oh, Emma, stop apologizing and tell me about this shooting case."

So Emma rallied and told him the little she had heard and all she had read in the morning's papers.

"Now, that is odd," said Charles. "It's all so neat and tidy. Is Agatha at the office?"

"No, we all have the weekend off."

"But you said you were working."

"I'm conscientious."

"I'd better drop in on Aggie."

Emma simpered. "Today might not be a good time. She has a young man staying with her."

"That'll be the dreadful Roy. I'd better get over there. If she had let me in on it, I'd never have let her leave it until the morning. Now look what's happened. Nice to see you, Emma, but I'll let you get on with your work. Gustav!"

The door opened. "What?"

"Show Mrs. Comfrey out."

Emma followed Gustav out and through the shadowy hall. "Phone next time," said Gustav and slammed the great door behind her.

She got into her car feeling very flat and diminished. She had better get home and look up the case files she was working on, select a missing cat or dog and say it had been reported in Warwickshire. Emma switched on the engine and let in the clutch and drove slowly off, her dreams crumbling about her ears. But when she reached the bottom of the drive, she remembered with a sudden glow that he had called her glamorous. And he had felt so at ease with her that he had not bothered to dress.

By the time she had turned into Lilac Lane, her fantasies were back in full force. She must call on Agatha when Charles arrived. But first she must come up with a case as an excuse for visiting him.

Having found what she considered a good enough excuse, she sat on a chair on the landing by the side window overlooking the entrance to Agatha's cottage. Agatha's car was not there. Emma prayed that Charles would arrive before Agatha returned. That way she could nip out and invite him into her cottage to wait. She was just wrapped in a rosy fantasy where Charles was saying, "I feel so comfortable here with you, Emma. Makes me realize what a lonely life I've had," when she heard the sound of a car.

Charles drove up and took a bag out of the boot and headed for the door. But instead of ringing, he took out a set of keys, selected one, opened the door and went in.

Emma bit her thumb. Well, she had been going to call on

Agatha, hadn't she? No harm in ringing the bell. She went to the bathroom and repaired her make-up, patted her hair and went next door. She rang the bell.

Charles was sprawled on the sofa watching a rerun of *Frasier.* He heard the bell but decided not to answer it. Probably some boring woman from the village.

Emma retreated, baffled.

Frasier being finished, Charles decided to visit Mrs. Bloxby to pass the time until Agatha returned.

Emma, now downstairs, saw him pass the window. She rushed towards her front door, but tripped over a footstool and went sprawling. When she had picked herself up and opened her door, there was no sign of him. She set off in pursuit, out of Lilac Lane and past the general stores. There, ahead of her, turning off from the main street down the cobbled lane which led to the church, was Charles.

There's no service today, thought Emma, so he must be going to call on Mrs. Bloxby.

She drew back a little. Let him get inside the vicarage and then she could stroll casually up and ring the bell. Mrs. Bloxby would not think it strange. Everyone in the village called on Mrs. Bloxby. She would wait for five minutes.

"It's good of you to let me in," Charles was saying.

"Why should I not let you in?"

"It was just when I rang your doorbell," said Charles, "that I suddenly realized how irritating people can be when they just land up on your doorstep without telephoning and expect a welcome."

"Were you thinking about anyone specific?"

"That Emma Comfrey who works for Agatha. Rolled up this morning at my home."

"Oh dear. You haven't *encouraged* her in any way, have you?"

"I took her out for lunch a couple of times. But she's old enough, just, to be my mother."

"Come into the garden. We'll have coffee there."

Charles relaxed in the pleasant vicarage garden under the shade of an old cedar. The sun blazed down. As Mrs. Bloxby prepared the coffee, there was a comforting tinkle of china from the kitchen and a smell of warm scones. Up on the hill a tractor crossed a field, looking like a toy.

The doorbell rang.

Charles stiffened as he heard the door open and Mrs. Bloxby say loudly, "Why, Mrs. Comfrey."

Charles shot to his feet, feeling suddenly hunted. He vaulted nimbly over the garden wall into the churchyard and hid behind a sloping gravestone.

"He was here a minute ago," he heard Mrs. Bloxby say. "He must have remembered something and just left. I'm sure you can catch him if you hurry."

Charles stayed where he was until he heard Mrs. Bloxby calling, "You can come out now."

Charles climbed back over the garden wall and brushed down his trousers.

"Coffee's ready," said Mrs. Bloxby placidly.

Charles grinned as he sat down at the garden table. "I didn't know you were capable of lying."

"I didn't lie. I said you had left and so you had. Mrs. Comfrey has blonded her hair and is wearing full make-up. What have you done?"

"I was only being kind to the old bird. She's had a rough life. Never mind her. I'm waiting for Aggie to get back to tell me all about the shooting."

Emma waited on her chair on the landing. She saw Roy and Agatha return, and then Charles came strolling along Lilac Lane.

Once more she decided to wait five minutes and then go and join them.

She kept glancing down at her watch. How slow the second hand crawled around the dial! At last, she straightened up, went downstairs and marched next door.

Agatha opened the door. "Why, Emma. What can I do for you?"

"I thought I might join you for a coffee."

"I'm afraid now is not a good time," said Agatha firmly. "You've got the whole weekend off, Emma. Make the most of it. I'll see you in the office on Monday."

Emma marched back to her own cottage, back ramrod-straight, and two spots of angry colour burning in her cheeks.

She hated Agatha Raisin. Agatha must have sensed Charles's growing interest in her and was jealously keeping him to herself.

"That was Emma," said Agatha, joining Roy and Charles in the garden. "But I couldn't ask her in because I want to tell you about the case and Emma mustn't know about us finding the body before the police. So where was I? Oh, yes, the more I think about that suicide, the more worried I get."

"Say it wasn't suicide," said Roy. "Who's the murderer?

Jason is in Bermuda, although he's probably heading back by now. Laggat-Brown has a cast-iron alibi. Who's left?"

"Someone we don't know about," suggested Charles. "Might be an idea to get hold of Harrison Peterson's wife."

"I could phone Patrick," said Agatha reluctantly. "But I told him to take a rest."

"You could see if he's dug up anything else and then he can rest while we do something about it," said Charles.

Roy shifted uneasily in his chair. He resented the appearance of Charles, although he knew him of old. This was supposed to *his* weekend with Agatha.

"While you make your phone calls," he said. "I'll take a walk down the village."

"Right," said Agatha. "I'll phone Patrick."

Roy nipped upstairs and changed out of his white suit into an old pair of jeans, checked shirt and moccasins. He could see no reason to waste the glory of his best wardrobe on what he waspishly damned as "a bunch of sheep-shaggers."

He was just strolling past the cottage next door when Emma, who had been pretending to weed her front garden, called out, "Are you visiting Agatha?"

"Yes," said Roy, "but she's got phone calls to make and I'm feeling bored."

"Why don't you come in and we'll sit in my garden and have coffee."

Roy brightened. "Just until she's finished with her phone calls."

He followed her through her cottage, looking about him as he passed through the living room. It had changed a lot since the days of James Lacey, Agatha's ex. Where James had walls lined with books, Emma had shelves of ornaments: china cats, little pottery houses and glass animals. The wood-burning fire now had an electric fire with fake logs in front of it. A sofa and armchairs were covered in chintz. Roy thought it all charming.

"Now sit down," said Emma brightly when they were in the garden, "and I'll fetch the coffee. I'll just move this umbrella so that you're in the shade. It is rather hot."

Nice old bird, thought Roy, stretching his feet out on the grass.

Agatha came back from the phone. "He's working on the wife's address, but I've got the doctor's. It's a Dr. Singh in Cheltenham. His surgery's in Portland Lane just off the old Bath Road."

"He won't be there on Saturday. He might have an emergency surgery on Saturday mornings, but it'll be over by now. You think someone else got these sleeping pills masquerading as Peterson?"

"Far-fetched, I know," said Agatha, "but I'd like to check it out. I'm hungry. I'll make us something to eat."

"No, you don't. Last time I was here it was the Swami's extra-hot curry done in the microwave. We'll get something in Cheltenham."

"All right. We'll drive round the village and pick up Roy."

But there was no sign of the young man. He was not in the Red Lion or in the general stores or anywhere walking along the cobbled sun-baked streets.

"Let's just go without him," said Agatha.

"You'd better leave a note," said Charles. "You've got a nasty way of cutting out your friends when it suits you."

Agatha opened her mouth to apologize to Charles for having left him when she had gone with Patrick for lunch, but the apology died on her lips.

They drove back to Lilac Lane where Agatha scribbled a note for Roy and propped it on the kitchen table against a jar of instant coffee.

"I'd better get back," Roy was saying reluctantly. "Maybe they've found out the address of that doctor."

"What doctor's that?" asked Emma.

"Well, Harrison Peterson took an overdose of sleeping pills, so they want to check up and make sure he really got them for himself."

Emma saw her chance. "I'll come with you," she said. "I am a detective, too."

"Good idea," said Roy. Emma had mothered him and fussed over him, something, he thought, that Agatha Raisin should learn how to do.

They went next door. There was no answer to the doorbell. Agatha had completely forgotten that Roy did not have a key.

Roy turned round. "Her car's here but his has gone. I must say that's a bit thick. And I'm hungry. Tell you what, I'll take you for lunch."

Emma brightened. This young man was obviously attracted to much older women. Although her heart ached for the missing Charles, it was flattering to be escorted around by Roy.

Roy's boss, on hearing that he was going to visit Agatha, had suggested that he try to lure her back to London to do some free-lance work. Roy knew he could take Emma out for a slap-up lunch and put it on his expense sheet as having entertained Agatha.

They drove into Oxford and parked at the Randolph Hotel.

He hoped people would think Emma was his mother. She looked such a lady. She looked like the type of woman one always wanted one's mother to look like on school sports day. He remembered his own mother with a shudder. She'd been such a coarse, powerful woman.

Over lunch, Emma began a tale of her miserable life. Most of Emma's life had indeed been pretty miserable, but a lot of it had been self-inflicted. She had taken revenge on people who had upset her at the office by spreading false rumours about them. She had nearly lost her job once. A pretty secretary had been rising up the ranks fast. She was popular with everyone. In a fit of spite, Emma had squeezed a tube of Superglue over the keyboard of her computer after erasing all the girl's files.

As some of the files contained classified documents, the police forensic department had been called in. Emma had worn gloves, but someone had seen her coming out of the girl's office, and although nothing could be proved against her, she had ended her years at the Ministry of Defence under a cloud. She still felt that it had been an extraordinary fuss about nothing. The files had been restored from the hard drive and a new keyboard found.

But of course she did not tell Roy about that particular crime. Roy listened, fascinated. Although Emma had been only a secretary, she told Roy that she had been a spy, sent to different countries on dangerous missions. She invented several colourful stories.

Then she realized that if Roy told Agatha or Charles anything about these stories, she might not be believed, and so she said, "Please don't tell Agatha or Charles anything about my secret life. I shouldn't have told you. But you are such a good listener, and"—she giggled—"such a very attractive young man."

Roy beamed. He wished he had worn his white suit.

SIX

✝

"WE'RE in luck," said Charles. "God bless the Asians. He's got a surgery at two o'clock this afternoon. We'll have a quick bite to eat. How are we going to handle this? Ask him outright? Or are you going to pretend to be ill and then drop it into the conversation?"

"Ask him outright. I'll phone Roy. I feel guilty about him." Agatha rang her home number but there was no reply.

They had a sandwich in a pub and then went back to the surgery. There were already five people waiting. Agatha went up to the receptionist and handed her card over. "We would like a few words with Dr. Singh."

The receptionist was an enormous woman. Her thighs spilled over the typing chair. Her huge bosom cast a shadow over the keyboard in front of her. Her head was surprisingly small despite triple chins. Agatha guessed she could not be any more than thirty years old. Her appearance conjured up memories of a seaside holiday where one got one's photograph taken by sticking one's head through a life-sized cardboard cut-out of the fairground's fat lady.

"You'll need to wait until all the patients have been seen to," she said. "Take a seat."

So they did and waited and waited. Agatha tried to contact Roy several times, phoning Roy's mobile phone as well as her own home number, but failing each time to get a reply.

At last they were told that Dr. Singh would see them. Dr. Singh was a small neat man, dark-skinned, wearing glasses and a white coat, as thin as his receptionist was fat.

"I have already spoken to the police," he began. "I see you are a private detective, Mrs. Raisin. I assume you wish to ask about the sleeping pills I was supposed to have prescribed."

"Yes," said Agatha eagerly.

"Mr. Harrison Peterson was a temporary patient. He suffered from high blood pressure. I prescribed high blood pressure pills. The police showed me the bottle. Someone had carefully extracted a label from another bottle, a bottle of barbiturates, steamed off the label—I should guess—on the bottle of high blood pressure medicine and then replaced it with the part that stated the medicine was sleeping pills. Then they pasted on the section with my name and the name of the pharmacy."

"So it must have been murder," said Charles.

Outside, Agatha said excitedly, "So the case is open again. How did the murderer get him to take the sleeping pills?"

"Can't think. I wonder what the results of the autopsy were," said Charles as they walked to the car-park. "I mean, he may not have taken sleeping pills. He knew his killer. No sign of forced entry. They have a drink. The murderer doctors Peterson's drink with that date-rape drug, whatever it's called, and then, when he passes out, smothers him with a pillow or pinches his nostrils and then sets the scene."

"You know what this means? We're back at the beginning," mourned Agatha, "and I don't know where to start."

"Phone Patrick and see if he's got an address for the wife."

Agatha phoned Patrick and told him what they had found out. Then Charles heard her say excitedly, "You've found the wife? Where is she? Hang on a minute."

Holding the phone under her ear, she took a notebook and pen out of her bag and wrote something down. "I'll go and see her," said Agatha. "The murderer was obviously someone that Peterson knew."

When she rang off, she said to Charles, "She's living in Telegraph Road in Shipston-on-Stour."

"I think we should go back and get Roy," said Charles cautiously. "He must be feeling a bit neglected."

"I'll try him again," said Agatha. Again she tried her home number and Roy's mobile phone number without success.

"He's not sitting waiting for us," she said. "Let's just go and see this wife. It won't take long."

"It's too bad of Agatha to leave you like this," Emma was saying.

Roy shrugged. "She might have been trying to phone me but I left my mobile on the table beside the bed."

"Why don't you phone her?"

"I forget her mobile number all the time. Now that's in my address book on the table beside the bed as well. You don't have it, do you?"

Emma had one of Agatha's cards with both home and mobile number on it. If she gave it to Roy, Agatha might come back with dear Charles. On the other hand, the longer she stayed away and the angrier Roy got, the more Agatha would be shown up in a bad light. Anything that might disaffect Charles as well was all to the good.

Roy was sitting in Emma's living-room. He glanced out of the window and saw Agatha's cleaner, Doris Simpson, walking past.

He shot up. "Mrs. Simpson. I'd forgotten about her. She'll have a key."

He rushed out, followed by Emma.

An hour later, at Moreton-in-Marsh station, Roy said, "You've been awfully kind to me, Emma. No, don't bother walking over the bridge with me." He kissed her on the cheek.

The opposite platform across the bridge was already full of people waiting for the London train. Clutching his travel bag, Roy strode off towards the bridge, thinking that anyone watching would be sure that Emma was his mother.

Emma watched him go and felt a little frisson of delightful naughtiness. She felt sure anyone watching would think that Roy was her young lover.

"Here's Telegraph Road and a convenient car-park." Charles turned into the car-park and stopped.

Agatha opened the passenger door and got out, wincing slightly as she did so.

"Rheumatism?" asked Charles.

"No," snapped Agatha. "Just a slight cramp."

Agatha had been aware for several weeks now of a nagging

pain in her hip. But her mind shrieked against the very idea of her having rheumatism or arthritis. Those were ailments of the elderly, surely.

Joyce Peterson lived in a small cottage that leaned slightly towards the road.

Agatha's hand hovered over the bell. "I wonder why she wasn't invited to her son's engagement party."

"Ring the bell," said Charles. "You'll never find out if you don't ask."

"Why do I never phone first?" mourned Agatha.

"Because you're an amateur." Charles's voice had an unfamiliar edge to it.

Agatha was just turning to stare at him in surprise when the door opened. A tall blonde woman answered the door. She was wearing tight jeans and a white shirt tied round her trim waist. Her beautiful, expressionless face was half hidden by a wing of her hair.

"Is Mrs. Peterson at home?"

"I am Mrs. Peterson, or was. What do you want?"

Agatha handed over her card. "We are investigating the murder of your husband."

"Murder! But I was told it was suicide!"

"Please, may we come in? I am Agatha Raisin and this is Sir Charles Fraith. We'll tell you all about it."

She nodded and turned away. They followed her through a kitchen and into a long airy room at the back. Agatha was amazed. From the outside, the cottage looked as if it would not have any significant space at all. The room had obviously been extended out to take space from the long garden at the back.

It was tastefully furnished, a mixture of modern and some good antiques.

Joyce sat in an armchair by the open French windows. A gentle breeze floated in, bringing with it the scent of late roses from the garden. Charles and Agatha sat on a sofa opposite her.

She did not ask any questions, simply waited in silence.

Agatha explained how they had found out about the sleeping pills. Still, Joyce said nothing.

"Why weren't you invited to your son's engagement party?" asked Charles.

"I was invited but I preferred not to go. Much as I love my son, he said some unforgivable things when I divorced his father. I met the Laggat-Brown female once. Detestable woman. Jason crawls to her. Cassandra is all right, but silly and empty-headed."

"Why did you divorce your husband?" asked Agatha.

"Why not? You mean I should have stood by a jailbird? He was charged with not only insider trading but pocketing money from clients' accounts. Then there was another woman."

"Who?"

"I don't know. But I checked his credit-card bills one day. There was a diamond necklace from Asprey's, hotels and meals in Paris, perfume, clothes, all that. When I challenged him, he said the Paris trips were business and the presents were for clients. I was going to divorce him even if he hadn't gone to prison. Prison simply made the divorce proceedings easier."

"Did he know Mr. Laggat-Brown?" asked Charles.

"If he did, he never mentioned it."

"What kind of man was your husband?"

The room was growing dark and there came a faint rumble of thunder in the distance.

"When I met him, he was very charming. A high-flyer. I like

the good things of life. Then I had Jason. He was such a darling little boy."

"You must have been married very young," said Charles.

"I was eighteen. I wanted to keep the boy at home, but by the time he was eight, Harrison insisted he was sent away to prep school and then Winchester. He began to change. Very much his father's boy. Little time for me."

A sudden puff of wind lifted the wing of hair back from her face, and in the lamplight they saw her cheek was marred by a large bruise.

"That's a nasty bruise," said Charles.

"Silly of me," she said. "I didn't notice a cupboard door in the kitchen was open and walked right into it."

There came the rattle of a key in the front door and a man's voice called, "Joyce!"

"In here, dear."

A tall man carrying a briefcase walked into the room. He was well-built and tanned with very light grey eyes. He was wearing a well-cut business suit.

"Mark, these people are detectives. They say that Harrison was murdered."

Those eyes of his, as cold as chips of ice, fastened on Agatha and Charles. "You're not the police, so get out of here."

"But Mark—"

"Shut up. You two. Out!"

"You'd better go." Joyce's voice sounded weary.

Agatha turned in the doorway. "You have my card. If there's anything I can do . . ."

"Just go."

"Isn't it amazing," said Charles as they hurried to the car-park just as fat drops of rain were beginning to fall. "They marry one bastard, then as soon as they're free, they marry another. I'll never understand women."

"I've just remembered something." Agatha slid into the passenger seat. "I forgot to leave Roy a key. That's why he didn't answer any of my calls."

"Oh, Aggie. Of all the things. You'll just need to hope he's found refuge with Mrs. Bloxby."

In Agatha's cottage, there were two notes on the kitchen table. One was from Doris Simpson saying she had let the cats out after feeding them. The other was from Roy. "I don't know what you think you're playing at, you old bat, but if it hadn't been for Emma I would have had a rotten time. Doris Simpson finally let me in. I'm off to London. No point in staying. Roy."

"Snakes and bastards," muttered Agatha.

"Your trouble," said Charles, who had read the note over her shoulder, "is that now you're running around being a professional detective, you think your friends are to be picked up and left at will."

The doorbell rang. "You get it, Charles," said Agatha. "I'll try Roy on his mobile."

Charles opened the door. Emma stood there, fresh makeup, golden trouser suit, shielded from the rain under a golfing umbrella.

"Oh, come in," said Charles. "Agatha's on the phone."

He led the way into the kitchen.

"Can I get you something?"

"No, I'm all right, Charles. I've been thinking. I owe you not one but two lunches. My turn next."

And she gazed at Charles with simple adoration in her eyes.

Alarm bells went off in Charles's head. "That's very kind of you, Emma, but I'm afraid I have to leave. Got things to attend to."

Emma's face fell. Agatha came into the kitchen. "Oh, it's you, Emma. Thank you for looking after, Roy. He's been singing your praises."

"Has he forgiven you?" asked Emma.

"Oh, yes," said Agatha and Charles noticed a flicker of disappointment in Emma's eyes.

Agatha had mollified Roy by promising to travel up to London and buy him the best meal in town.

"Isn't it a pity," said Emma brightly. "Charles has just told me he is leaving."

Agatha's bearlike eyes focused on Charles. "But we've got so much to find out."

"Sorry, Aggie. Got to go. I haven't unpacked my bag, so I'll be off."

"I'd better go, too," said Emma, anxious to hang on to Charles until the very last minute.

"Can't I persuade you to stay?" asked Agatha, following them to the door.

"Sorry." Charles picked up his bag and kissed her on the cheek.

He walked out to his car with Emma following. "Goodbye," she said, turning her cheek towards him for a kiss. Charles pretended not to notice. He slung his bag in the boot and then got into the driver's seat.

Emma walked to her cottage and stood on the doorstep, waving and waving until his car had turned the corner of Lilac Lane and disappeared.

Agatha felt forlorn.

Charles drove down to Moreton-in-Marsh and parked by the war memorial. He took out his mobile phone and called Agatha. "Feel like dinner?"

"Yes, but I thought you'd gone!"

"I'm parked by the war memorial in Moreton. Come down and collect me and I'll tell you about it."

Over a pub dinner, Agatha exclaimed again, "I can't believe it. Emma!"

"That's the reason for the new hairdo and the new clothes."

"Emma's such a simple, friendly person. Surely you must be mistaken."

"No, I'm not. She could be dangerous."

"How?"

"I just feel uneasy about it. I'll creep back with you. I'm sure she goes to bed early. You haven't really talked much about Laggat-Brown, now that we're on the subject of romance."

"I had dinner with him and he seemed very pleasant."

"He's my prime suspect."

"Come on, Charles. He's got a cast-iron alibi and he wouldn't want to murder his own daughter. It's obvious he adores her. My money's on Jason. He's the only one with a motive."

"But to kill his own father! Wait a bit. That's out. He was in Bermuda."

"So he was. We seem to be going round and round."

"What about Joyce Peterson's new squeeze? Maybe he's fanatically jealous of the ex and wanted revenge. Maybe he meant to shoot Jason. You know, Aggie, if it hadn't been for that death threat, we wouldn't be in such a muddle. What if the death threat was a blind? What if the intended target wasn't Cassandra? Don't you see, she's the stumbling block. As long as we keep looking on Cassandra as the intended victim, we'll get nowhere. So let's take Jason as a possible."

"Can't see why," Agatha said.

"What about Mrs. Laggat-Brown?"

"Possible. Husband's in the clear. What about the Felliets?"

"I know George very well and I can't imagine him doing anything murderous."

"What about the daughter? She might know something about the Laggat-Browns."

"I never met her. I believe Felicity is very beautiful."

"It's a long shot. Could you phone Sir George and ask if he now knows where she is?"

"He'll wonder why we're asking. I think I should drop along to Ancombe tomorrow and ask him in the way of conversation. Say I happened to be passing by."

Emma heard the sound of a car turning into Lilac Lane and ran upstairs to the landing and looked out.

Charles and Agatha got out. They were laughing at something. At me? thought Emma, and put her arms across her body and hugged herself in a paroxysm of jealousy.

In that moment, she hated Agatha Raisin. As she prepared herself for bed that night and then lay down under the duvet, she fantasized that with Agatha out of the way, Charles would turn to her. He obviously had a penchant for older women. If Agatha was killed during an investigation, no one would ever think of Emma. Of course, she wouldn't actually do it. Would she?

*   *   *

Charles strolled through Ancombe the next morning. Agatha had driven him down to Moreton to collect his car. She had gone off to the office and he had decided to drive to Ancombe, park his car a little ways from where the Felliets lived and see if he could bump into George as if by accident.

He went into the general stores to buy cigarettes. He rarely smoked, usually preferring to "borrow" a cigarette from someone else, but this was one of the rare days when he really wanted a smoke.

As he entered the store, he heard the woman behind the counter saying, "That'll be seven pounds and fifty pee, Lady Felliet."

Charles forgot about the cigarettes. What was her first name? Something odd. Crystal, that was it.

He moved forward as Lady Felliet turned away from the counter. "It's Crystal, isn't it?"

She was a tall woman. He remembered she had been a blonde beauty when he used to go to deb dances in his early twenties. The blonde was now streaked with grey and worn in a knot at the back of her neck. Her hazel eyes were still beautiful, but two hard lines scored down either side of a mouth that had a discontented droop. She was wearing a tweed suit that had seen better days over a silk blouse, thick stockings and serviceable walking shoes.

"Who are you?" she demanded.

"Charles Fraith."

"Charlie? Of course it's you. Good heavens. George told me you'd called round the other day. What brings you here?"

"I'm staying with a friend in Carsely. Went out for a drive and suddenly felt I wanted a cigarette."

"Get your cigarettes and come home for coffee. We don't see many people these days."

Charles bought a packet of Bensons and joined her again. "It wasn't so bad in the beginning," said Crystal. "Oh, thank you." Charles had taken the shopping basket from her. "I really should get one of those carts on wheels. But so naff."

"Not any more," said Charles. "What were you saying about the old days?"

"Well, not so far back. I make it sound like centuries. But that's what it feels like sometimes. When we first moved here, we got invited for weekend house parties and things. People, however, do expect one to return hospitality. I gave a few dinner parties in our poky little cottage, but it didn't work and finally the invitations stopped coming. I hate that Laggat-Brown creature."

"Wasn't her fault you lost your money, though."

"True. But I mean the feelings of humiliation. She did crow over one. Here we are. George will be delighted."

George did look pleased to see Charles. "Do you mind if I leave you boys to your coffee?" said Crystal. "I really must do some gardening."

"Go ahead. I'll make the coffee," said George.

Charles followed him into the kitchen and waited while George boiled the kettle and put spoonfuls of instant coffee in two mugs. Charles recognized it as the cheapest instant coffee that could be bought.

"Right," said George. "Grab your mug, old man, and follow me through."

When they were seated, he went on, "I do feel sorry for Crystal. All this scrimping and saving is getting to her."

"You could get a job," said Charles.

George goggled at him. "No one will employ me at my age."

"You're only . . . what? Forty-four?"

"Forty-five. And where could I work?"

"Tesco's supermarket at Stow are always advertising for staff."

"My dear fellow, can you see me on the till? Crystal would die of shame."

"They need people at supermarkets to stack the shelves. Or what about these all-night garages? They're always looking for someone. It would pay your grocery bills. Doesn't your daughter help out?"

"Felicity has expensive tastes. I really don't think she has anything left over at the end of the month."

"What is she doing again?"

"Working as personal assistant to some couturier."

"Where?"

"In Paris, where else? Rue Saint-Honoré."

"Which couture house?"

"You do ask a lot of questions. Thierry Duval. Have you seen his fashions? Weird. Saw them on the telly. And the way the models have to walk these days. Just as if they'd wet their knickers."

"When did you last see her?"

"Last Christmas. She came over. Seems to enjoy the work."

"I'd like to see a photograph of her."

"What's all this interest in Felicity? She's too young for you, Charles."

Charles's eyes swivelled around the room and came to rest on a studio photograph of a beautiful blonde. She had been photographed looking straight at the camera and leaning on her hands, à la Princess Di.

He pointed. "That's her, isn't it?"

"Yes, so what? Honestly, old man, you've changed. Can't remember you firing questions at one the whole bloody time."

"Sorry," said Charles and began to chatter lightly about people they both knew, lacing it with enough scurrilous gossip that George forgot about all those strange questions and looked sorry when Charles said he had to leave.

Agatha was lucky in that the police, sure that Harrison Peterson's death had been a suicide, had not ordered an intensive forensic search of the room and the stairs leading to it. By the time they got around to it, the room and the stairs had been scrubbed clean and the room itself had a new tenant. She had been worried about their footprints on the stairs or a stray one of her hairs somewhere in the room.

Emma was being singularly sweet to Agatha that morning. Agatha must never guess what she, Emma, had planned for her, although she reminded herself from time to time that it was only a fantasy to dispel her jealousy and rage.

Charles came into the office during the morning and gave Agatha his report of Felicity Felliet. He had decided not to bother explaining to Emma why he was still around. "Paris, again," said Agatha. "I wonder what she was doing the night of the party."

"We could run over and ask her. Plane there, plane back. One day should do it."

Emma dug her newly painted fingernails into her hands. The pair of them in romantic Paris!

"What about tomorrow?" asked Agatha.

"It'll need to be the day after. I'm hosting the village fête at the house. Anyway, what now?"

"I think we should try to catch Bill Wong. See if he can tell us anything more. What are you doing, Emma? What about that missing cat, Biggles?"

"Just about to go out on it," said Emma.

Bill Wong saw them in one of the interviewing rooms. "I hope you have something to tell me," he said. "I'm not supposed to help private detectives."

"We heard a rumour that Harrison Peterson's death was murder," said Agatha.

"Nothing's in the papers yet," said Bill. "Where did you hear that?"

"I can't tell you that, Bill."

"Then I can't tell you anything either."

"Probably because you don't know anything," said Charles.

"Look." Bill surveyed both of them. "Wilkes happened to be around when I got the message that you wanted to see me. He told me to get rid of you, fast. On the other hand, I'll be in the Wheatsheaf at lunch-time."

"See you there. Come along, Charles."

As Emma trudged around the streets of Mircester, looking for the missing Biggles, she turned over what Charles had said that morning. He was hosting a village fête. She could mingle with the crowds and watch him and see if there was any other female he was interested in. She had read up on him in the local newspapers and learned that he had been married to a Frenchwoman and was now divorced.

It would be better fun than looking for this cat. Agatha had two cats. Emma was beginning to hate cats.

She turned into the street where Biggles's owner lived. Emma peered over the hedge into the garden. Biggles was sunning himself on the lawn. She thought quickly. She knew the owner, a widow, Mrs. Porteous, would be out at work.

Emma opened the garden gate and pounced on the sleeping cat. She thrust it into the cat carrier she was carrying with her. She decided to take Biggles home with her. He could be considered missing for another day and that would give her time to go to the fête. It was amazing how many cat owners didn't just wait for their precious animals to reappear.

She put the carrier with the now angry cat in the back of her car, which she had parked a few streets away. Then she wondered uneasily if Mrs. Porteous knew her cat had returned and had left it out in the garden while she went to work. Emma flipped open her address book and found the work number and dialled.

"This is Emma Comfrey," she said. "Just to let you know we're still looking."

"Oh, bless you," said Mrs. Porteous. Her voice became quavery. "I worry the whole time about him. I fear he might be dead."

"There, there," said Emma. "I'm working all day long looking for him."

Bill Wong had nothing to tell them that they didn't know already. But they were able to tell him about Joyce Peterson's violent partner.

"She didn't tell us she was living with anyone," said Bill. "We had a devil of a job tracing her. How did you catch up with her?"

"Someone told us."

"I wonder who that someone was. Anyway, you say this Mark is violent. What gave you that idea?"

"She had an enormous bruise on her cheek. She said she had walked into an open cupboard door, which is a battered woman's variation on the theme of 'I fell downstairs'."

"We'd better check him out. Got a second name for him?"

"No, just Mark. He might have killed Harrison Peterson in a jealous rage."

"I hope not," said Bill.

"Why?"

"Because that would mean that we would still be left with the shooting at the Laggat-Browns. This Mark would have no reason to want to kill the daughter. It's one of those cases that's going to drag on and on. I haven't had time to do anything in the garden, and despite last night's rain, it's as dry as a bone. Do you think there's something in this global warming business?"

Said Charles, "It was evidently as hot as hell in medieval times. Give it another hundred or so years and we'll have another mini ice age."

"What now?" asked Charles after they had said goodbye to Bill.

"Paris, I suppose. While you're playing lord of the manor at your fête, I'll take a day off and run up to London and take Roy out."

"Shouldn't you be doing some work?"

"I've got staff. Why keep a kennelful of dogs and bark myself?"

Emma's face lit up when Agatha said she was going up to London to see Roy on the following day.

"Such a dear boy," she said, and added coyly, "Give him my love."

"Will do."

With Agatha out of the road, thought Emma, she could deliver the pesky cat to its grateful owner and have the whole day free.

SEVEN

†

WHAT had happened to London? Agatha wondered, and not for the first time. Had the streets always been so dirty? Perhaps if she were living in London again, she would not notice.

She took Roy to the Caviar Restaurant in Piccadilly. Agatha did not like caviar and thought it a waste of money, but she was anxious not to lose Roy's friendship and knew that the very prices on the menu would delight him.

Roy listened carefully while she told him that Peterson had been murdered.

"There's been nothing in the papers," said Roy. He was wearing a very conventional business suit, shirt and tie.

"Probably the police are keeping it quiet. Honestly, I've been going over everything in my head."

"The murderer must have been someone Peterson knew," said Roy, spooning up caviar, and hoping the people walking along Piccadilly on the other side of the large plate-glass window were envying him. "I mean, you didn't say anything about the door of his room being forced. He must have phoned someone else besides you. How else could anyone have found out? Unless your phone is bugged."

"You've been reading too many spy stories."

"Believe me, I have recently been talking to a real-life spy, and truth is stranger than fiction."

"What real-life spy?"

"Oh, just someone I met. I'm not supposed to talk about it. Have they buried the body?"

"I don't think so. There'll be another autopsy if the police think anything could have been missed in the first one."

"Might be worth your while to look into that boyfriend of Joyce Peterson's. He sounds a violent sort of chap."

"I might call on her tomorrow when I know he's out at work. But I don't think so. I mean, someone had a very sophisticated sniper rifle. You'd almost think someone was being paid to do it."

"You mean, like a professional assassin?"

"Yes, something like that."

"Can I have lobster?"

"Have anything you like."

"Emma's quite a dear, isn't she?"

"Yes, she turned out to be a very good worker."

"Hidden depths, there."

"I don't think so," said Agatha Raisin, who prided herself on being a good judge of character. "I think what you see is what you get."

*   *   *

Emma parked her car in a field near Barfield House that had been turned into a temporary car-park for the day. She was wearing a wide floppy hat and sunglasses, which she considered sufficient disguise.

Stands were briskly selling home-made jams and jellies, cakes, home-made wine, wooden salad bowls, country clothes and second-hand books. There was no entrance fee, but programmes of events cost two pounds each. Emma studied the programme. There were to be choir singing a hundred-yard sprint, wellie throwing, ferret racing, dog and horse judging competitions and various other events. The wellie throwing was new to Emma, but she guessed it would be to see who could throw a wellington boot the farthest.

Emma felt thirsty and headed towards a large refreshment tent. Her heart beat quickly when she saw Charles. He was sitting at a table near the entrance, selling raffle tickets. She longed to go over to him but was frightened that if he recognized her she would need to think up another lie, and besides, he might tell Agatha she had been at the fête instead of working. She bought a cup of tea and then sat in a corner of the tent and watched him hungrily. It would be marvellous if she were there by his side, greeting people, hanging on to his arm.

A pretty girl came up to Charles. He stood up and kissed her enthusiastically on both cheeks, and then she took his place at the table while Charles went outside.

Emma finished her tea and followed. Charles went up to a platform overlooking a meadow and announced the start of the hundred-yard sprint. Emma stayed and watched while he judged event after event. The sun beat down and her legs began to ache. She turned around to see if there was somewhere she could sit down and keep Charles in view.

And then she saw a fortune-teller's tent.

Emma was a great believer in astrology, clairvoyants and fortune-tellers. Perhaps Madame Zora could tell her whether there was any hope with Charles.

Madame Zora was Gustav, and Gustav was in a bad temper. Normally fond of his employer, he decided that day that he hated him. The woman from the village who had volunteered to play Madame Zora had fallen ill and Charles had insisted Gustav get dressed up and play the part.

Emma had to wait in a queue. Gustav was a big success. As the day grew hotter and his temper higher, his predictions became more and more bizarre. Word spread around the fête and people became anxious to consult this outrageous fortune-teller.

At last it was Emma's turn. She pushed aside the flap and walked in. The tent was dark and so she removed her sunglasses. It was delightfully eerie, she thought. The tent was almost completely dark except for a scented candle burning on a small table in front of Madame Zora, whose face was shadowed by a colourful shawl over "her" head.

"Sit down," said Gustav. He recognized her as that batty female who had called on Charles unannounced. Now, what had Charles said about her? He had said, "Don't be too hard on her, Gustav. She thinks she's had a miserable life. Bullied by her husband and bullied at her work."

"Give me your right hand," said Gustav.

He affected to study it and then said, "You have had a very unhappy life. You had a bullying husband, but he is now dead.

Your colleagues at work did not appreciate you. But your life is about to change."

"How?" demanded Emma.

"There is a man much younger than you who interests you."

"Oh, yes!"

Now what? thought Gustav. Then he thought, why not make trouble for that Raisin female as well? He knew from Charles that Emma worked for Agatha Raisin.

"There is a woman who stands between you and your love. Let me see." He bent down and fished a crystal ball out of its box at his feet. He hadn't bothered using it before. He peered into it. "Yes, I see her. She is middle-aged with brown hair and small eyes. While she is around, you do not have any hope. No hope at all."

"No hope," echoed Emma in a quavering voice.

"No hope," said Gustav lugubriously.

"What shall I do?"

"The solution is in your hands. Now Madame Zora is tired and cannot see anything else. That will be ten pounds, please."

Emma was so shaken that she opened her wallet and paid up without a murmur.

After she had gone, Gustav put one pound in the collection box out of his pocket, the actual price he should have charged, and kept the tenner for himself.

Emma left the tent feeling shaken. A little voice of common sense was telling her it was all rubbish, but yet, Madame Zora had known about her past life and had described Agatha Raisin.

She decided to leave the fête. The day was unseasonably hot, and her feet and legs hurt.

The fantasy of "removing" Agatha slowly began to become a reality in her obsessed brain.

But she very nearly decided to forget about the whole thing when Agatha, returned from London, called on her that evening.

"I took the opportunity to visit my solicitor in London, Emma," said Agatha. "In case anything happens to me in the near future, I have decided to leave the detective agency to you."

"Oh, Agatha, how kind!"

"I know you're getting on in years, and if nothing happens to me in, say, the next five, I will cancel the codicil. You've done very good work for me, Emma."

And then she added, "I'd better get home and pack a bag. I'm off to Paris with Charles in the morning."

When she had gone, Emma sat with her hands tightly clenched. *She* should be the one going off to Paris with Charles. Agatha out of the way would mean the detective agency would be hers. Charles obviously liked detecting. They could solve cases together. But how to get rid of Agatha Raisin? It would need to look like an accident. Emma's head felt hot and feverish.

Agatha and Charles flew to Paris on an early plane and took a taxi from Charles de Gaulle Airport to the couturiers in the Rue Saint-Honoré. They handed over their cards and sat on gilt chairs in the salon and waited for Felicity.

At last a middle-aged woman entered the salon, holding their cards by the tips of her fingers.

"I am so sorry," she said, "Mees Felicity is not here."

"Where is she?" demanded Agatha, looking at the trim-figured Frenchwoman standing over her and wondering if there was such a thing as a bad figure in Paris.

"Mees Felicity is on the vacances."

"When is she due back?"

"Pardon?"

Charles said in impeccable French, "Where has Felicity gone on holiday and when do you expect her to return?"

She replied in rapid French while Agatha waited impatiently.

Again Charles spoke and rose to go. "What was that all about?" demanded Agatha.

"She's gone on holiday to somewhere in the south of France but she's expected back tomorrow. She's only been working with them a few months. Worked as a secretary before and they needed someone here with a knowledge of computers."

"Rats," said Agatha. "If we change our flights, we'll lose the money on the return trip."

"We could always get one of those el cheapo flights or Eurostar. Seems a shame to go back now we're here. And we may as well double-check Laggat-Brown's alibi."

"Oh, all right," said Agatha. "What hotel was he staying in? I've forgotten."

"The Hotel Duval on the Boulevard Saint-Michel. May as well check in for the night. Won't be too busy this time of year."

"I'll phone Emma and Miss Simms," said Agatha, "and tell her we'll be here another day."

Emma felt she couldn't bear it. She had to take some sort of action. She remembered that she had a container of rat poison she had brought from her old home. You weren't supposed to poison rats or mice any more because of some European Union regulation. You were supposed to trap them and then hit them on the head with a hammer or something. First she had to get into Agatha's house.

Agatha had told Emma to tell Doris to look after the cats for another day. Emma called on Doris Simpson and said, "I thought as I live next door, it would be easier for me to look after the cats and save you coming and going."

"That would be great," said Doris. "I'll come along with you and show you how to work the burglar alarm."

In possession of Agatha's keys, Emma said goodbye to Doris and went down to the shed at the bottom of her garden and took down the box of rat poison. She did not allow herself to stop and think about the enormity of what she was doing.

She went to Agatha's cottage and let herself in. She went through to the kitchen where Agatha's two cats, Hodge and Boswell, stared up at her. She shooed them out into the garden.

Emma took down a jar of instant coffee, tipped half of the granules of rat poison into it, being careful to wear gloves, and then screwed the lid back on.

She felt suddenly calm. She found tins of cat food and filled two bowls. After half an hour, she let the cats back in and then went back to her own cottage, forgetting to set the burglar alarm or to lock the back door. The deed was done.

The receptionist at the Hotel Duval said he remembered Mr. Laggat-Brown very well, particularly since the hotel had been closely questioned by the police. Mr. Laggat-Brown was a most charming man. He spoke French like a native. He gathered that the police had checked the airlines and that Mr. Laggat-Brown was known to have travelled back to England when he said he did.

Agatha asked if he knew where Mr. Laggat-Brown had gone after he had checked into the hotel. He had been out for two hours.

The receptionist said that Mr. Laggat-Brown had said something about going to a reunion.

Unfortunately, they had only one room. Madame and Monsieur would have to share. Madame said angrily that they would look for another hotel. She did not want to find herself renewing her amorous relations with Charles and doubted her own strength of will if she found herself in bed with him. Charles told her to stop behaving like an outraged virgin. He spoke in rapid French and then said, "Aggie, stop wittering. It's got twin beds."

After they had unpacked, they had lunch in a nearby restaurant. After lunch, Charles said that he felt tired after the dawn start and suggested going back to the hotel for a siesta.

Agatha did not think she would sleep and was startled to find it was early evening when she woke up.

They both went out for a long walk along the Seine as night descended on one of the world's most beautiful cities. The terraces of the restaurants were filling up with people stopping for a coffee or an apéritif after work.

"Look how slim everyone is," marvelled Agatha, "and they all walk as if they've got books on their heads. They must teach them deportment in French schools."

"The women look fabulous," said Charles and Agatha experienced a pang of jealousy. "Let's find a restaurant."

"There's quite a reasonable one at Maubert -Mutualité," said Agatha. "They have snacks and things. We had quite a big lunch."

The restaurant was crowded but they managed to find a table at the back. They ordered croques monsieurs and a decanter of the house wine.

Agatha became uneasily aware that someone was staring at

her and looked across the restaurant. With a sinking heart, she recognized Phyllis Hepper, a public relations officer she had known in her London days. Phyllis was a famous lush.

To Agatha's horror, Phyllis rose and came over to their table. "It's Agatha, isn't it?" she said.

"Phyllis," said Agatha, relieved the woman appeared to be sober. "What are you doing in Paris?"

"I got married to a Frenchman."

"This is Charles Fraith, Charles, Phyllis. Phyllis and I knew each other when I was working in London."

Phyllis laughed. "I'm surprised you recognized me. I must have been drunk the whole time."

"Well . . ."

"It doesn't matter. I was a terrible drunk," said Phyllis to Charles. "But I joined AA. I go to meetings, or réunions Alcooliques Anonymes, as they call them here in Paris."

"Your French must be very good."

"Not yet. I go to the English-speaking ones at the Quai D'Orsay. Quite a lot of French people go as well. There was this terrible raggy old drunk came in, but he got it and now you wouldn't recognize him. He looks so well and handsome. You must come and visit me. Here's my card."

Agatha said they were leaving the next day, but if she was ever back in Paris she would look Phyllis up.

After she had left, Charles said, "I thought it was supposed to be Alcoholics *Anonymous*."

"She must be very new in the programme. I met people like her in London. Just in, they wanted to tell the world."

They finished their decanter of wine and Charles ordered another, saying it would help them sleep. They chatted idly about previous cases and then Charles asked suddenly, "What about Emma?"

"What about her?"

"I think she's stalking me."

"Oh, Charles. Such male vanity."

"No, really. I was up on the platform at the fête and I looked across and I'd swear it was her. I asked Gustav and he said he'd told her fortune."

"What was Gustav doing telling her fortune?"

"The woman who was supposed to tell them fell ill and I made Gustav dress up and do it. He turned out to be a wow. People like being frightened and he told them such dire things."

"What did he tell Emma?"

"He said he felt sorry for her, so he'd given her the usual rubbish about meeting a tall, dark stranger."

"I'll have a word with Emma. Do you know I've put a codicil in my will, giving her the detective agency?"

"Oh, Aggie. Did you tell her?"

"Yes."

"Cancel it."

"I'll have a talk to her about trailing around after you. But what did you expect? You took her to lunch a couple of times. Maybe she's lonely."

"You obviously don't think much of my charms."

Agatha looked at him. Even in an open-necked blue shirt and blue chinos, he looked neat and impeccably barbered.

"Eat your food," she said.

Emma clutched her hair. What if Charles drank the coffee? And Doris would tell the police that she had given her the keys, so she would be first suspect. How stupid and crazy she had been. There was a ring at the doorbell. When she opened the door, Doris Simpson was standing there.

"I'd better take the keys back," she said. "My Bert, he points out that Agatha is paying me for looking after them cats and it's cheating on her to have you do it."

"I don't mind," pleaded Emma.

"I must have the keys," insisted Doris. "Where are they?"

Really, thought the cleaner, Mrs. Comfrey looks as if she's about to faint.

"Oh, there they are," said Doris, seeing the keys on a small table inside the door. She pushed past the trembling Emma and picked up the keys.

"I think it would be best," said Doris, who was about the only woman in the village who called Agatha by her first name, "if you didn't tell Agatha about me giving you the keys. I need all the money I can get these days and I wouldn't want her to go thinking I had cheated her."

"I won't breathe a word," said Emma passionately. "Not a word."

When Doris had gone, Emma sat down and hugged her thin figure. Then she rose and went down to the shed in the garden and collected the rat poison and buried it under the compost heap.

She decided she would wait and wait until she saw them return and follow them in. She would knock over that jar of coffee, sweep it up and take the contents away. Miss Simms would know when they were due back because Agatha kept in touch with her.

"Aren't you coming to bed with me?" asked Charles.

"No," said Agatha. "And I wish you wouldn't parade around the room naked. It's disconcerting."

Charles climbed into his bed with a sigh. "You're getting old, Aggie."

"No, I'm not," said Agatha furiously. "You're amoral, that's what you are."

"I'm the same as I've always been. Good night."

Agatha lay awake for some time. She had slept with Charles before—and enjoyed it. But their intimacy never seemed to affect Charles, and Agatha, in the past, had been left feeling that she had been used, that sex with her was like a drink or a cigarette to Charles.

But soon the amount of wine she had drunk lulled her off to sleep and down into uneasy dreams.

The man could not believe his luck. He had climbed over the fence into Agatha's garden and crept up to the kitchen door. The kitchen door was slightly open. Emma had forgotten to close it when she let the cats back in.

He eased in and began to search the house. No one here, he thought. Well, a job's a job. I'll wait here until she gets back. Two pairs of eyes gleamed at him in the darkness. "Damn cats," he muttered. But he was fond of cats, so he shooed them out into the garden and closed the door.

Where on earth was the woman? His informant had told him she would be back this evening. Still, it was only midnight. Better to wait.

In the moonlight streaming in through the window, he saw a jar of instant coffee beside the kettle. May as well have some of that, he thought, and keep myself awake.

Emma awoke at dawn, sitting fully dressed in an armchair. She could not remember having fallen asleep. She suddenly wondered if she had shut the back door of Agatha's cottage after she had let the cats in. She went out of her cottage and looked nervously around, but no one was about. She went up the side path of Agatha's cottage and round to the garden door and slumped in disappointment. Then she saw the cats in the garden.

But I'm sure I let them in, thought Emma. Putting on her gloves, she tried the door and to her relief it opened. She switched on the light. Then she let out a stifled scream. The kitchen smelt of vomit and a man was lying on the kitchen floor. There was a revolver on the table. She grabbed the jar of coffee and retreated to the door. She sped to her own cottage. She had an identical jar of instant coffee in her kitchen. She wiped it down with a cloth to get rid of fingerprints and hurried back to Agatha's with it and placed it on the counter. Then she took out a cloth and wiped away her footprints as she backed out of the door. Wait, Emma! screamed a voice in her brain. How did he get in? Doris will say she gave you the keys, surely, and you will be accused of letting some man into the cottage. He couldn't be anyone Agatha knew. Not wearing a black mask and with a revolver on the table. She picked up a rock from the rockery and smashed a pane of glass on the door. Why hadn't the burglar alarm gone off? I can't have set it, thought Emma. I'll reset it. That means I'll have to let myself out through the front of the house.

A cold determination had set in. She opened a cupboard under the stairs and found a hand vacuum cleaner that Agatha used for her car. She carefully vacuumed after herself to the front door and set the alarm, praying it wouldn't go off. It shouldn't go off because the glass was already broken. Then she remembered he must have drunk out of a cup. Should she leave it? Yes, she must. She couldn't bear to go back. The path round the side of the house was gravel, so she was sure she hadn't left any incriminating footprints when she arrived. She didn't have the keys but the locks clicked shut automatically. She took the vacuum with her.

Emma went home, got undressed and went to bed. Her last waking thought was that dear Charles would never know how she had saved his life.

Agatha was shaken awake at nine the following morning by Charles. "Get up," said Charles urgently. "The French police are downstairs and want to speak to you."

"What's the time?"

"Eleven o'clock. All that wine. We slept in. You didn't even hear the phone. Get dressed and I'll go down first and see what they want."

Agatha scrambled into her clothes, wondering what on earth had happened. When she went down to the reception area, it was to find two policemen and what she judged to be two French detectives.

"I'd better explain," said Charles, "because their English isn't very good. A man has been found dead in your kitchen in Carsely. He looks as if he's been poisoned."

"Who is it?"

"Blessed if I know. All they want at the moment is a timetable of when we arrived in Paris and where we were. I've told them everything and they can check it."

Charles turned away from her and launched into rapid French. One of the detectives replied. Agatha waited impatiently.

"Seems to have been an intruder. The pane of glass in the kitchen door was smashed. There was a black Balaclava on the table and a revolver. Someone was out to get you, Aggie. We're to wait at the commissariat."

He turned again and spoke to the detectives.

"He says we'd better pack our bags and check out. It looks as if it's going to be a long day."

One of the detectives spoke again. Charles translated, "We're to have breakfast if we want while they search our room."

Agatha nodded. It was one of the few times in her life when she felt speechless.

That morning, Emma watched at her window. At last, she saw Doris walking past. She waited for a scream, but all was silent. And then in the distance, she heard police sirens.

Emma jumped to her feet. She would rush next door and get into the house before they arrived. Then, if she had left any footprint unvacuumed, it wouldn't matter.

The front door was standing open. Emma went in. Doris emerged from the kitchen, her face ashen. "Don't go in there. There's a dead body."

"Who is it?"

"Some man I've never seen before."

"Let me have a look," said Emma, "I might recognize him."

She walked into the kitchen. She had not taken a close look

at him before. He was a stocky man with thick black hair. His face was so contorted that Emma could not judge what he had looked like normally.

Bill Wong was the first to arrive.

"Both of you get out of here immediately," he snapped. "Where's Agatha?"

"In Paris," said Emma.

"Do you know where she is staying?"

"Miss Simms will know."

"Mrs. Comfrey, you are walking all over the crime scene. I must ask you to leave."

"Certainly. Oh, what a shock." Emma burst into tears, her nerves stretched to the limit.

Doris led her away. Emma dabbed at her eyes, wondering desperately if she had covered everything. She had buried the coffee jar under the compost heap where she had put the rat poison. But if Doris told them that she had had the keys, they might come and search her cottage and garden.

"I've got to get back and make a statement," said Doris. "Will you be all right?"

Emma rallied. "I won't go to the office today. I'll do some gardening to take my mind off things."

Agatha and Charles waited all morning in a room in the commissariat. Their passports and airline tickets had been taken away from them.

"They'll ask us what we were doing in Paris," whispered Charles. "We'd better say we tried to call on Felicity because George is an old friend of mine. We'll say we just needed a break."

"By staying at the same hotel as Laggat-Brown stayed?"

"Well, Mrs. Laggat-Brown has employed you, so you can say you were double-checking his alibi."

"Okay. I wonder how long we've got to wait here."

The door opened and a French police inspector who spoke English came in. He handed them their passports and two airline tickets. "The English police say you must leave on the one o'clock flight for Heathrow. They have decided that it is important that you return to England. A police car will be waiting for you at Heathrow."

Charles looked at his watch. "We'd better get moving."

"A police car will take you to Charles de Gaulle."

On the road to the airport, Charles said uneasily, "Are you thinking what I'm thinking?"

"Which is?"

"The revolver and the black Balaclava. Agatha, do you think someone might have taken a hit out on you?"

"In the Cotswolds?"

"Think about it. Whoever fired at Cassandra had a first-class sniper rifle. That wasn't amateur stuff."

"This is getting scary. Let's hope he turns out to be a well-known burglar. But why didn't the burglar alarm work?"

Emma unearthed the rat poison and the coffee jar, put them in a bag, and took them out to her car. She had made a statement to the police, saying that she had slept soundly and had not heard a thing. She breathed a sigh of relief when she drove off. Doris would surely tell the police about her having had the keys to Agatha's cottage. She drove out onto the old Worcester Road and up to where she knew the council tip was. She put the bag containing the rat poison and the coffee jar into a container of general rubbish and heaved a sigh of relief.

Then she thought, there was really nothing to worry about now. They would think the man had broken in. It would be assumed that the burglar alarm was faulty. She suddenly felt ill as she remembered the dead body on the kitchen floor, and stopped the car, got out and was violently sick.

EIGHT

†

AGATHA and Charles were taken straight to Mircester Police Headquarters and put in an interviewing room.

Then Detective Inspector Wilkes appeared with another man whom he introduced as Detective Inspector William Fother of the Special Branch. Another man followed them into the room and leaned against a wall, his arms folded.

"What have the Special Branch got to do with this?" asked Agatha.

"We'll ask the questions," said Fother.

He was a dark-skinned man with thinning brown hair and large ugly hands which he folded on the table in front of him. His first question surprised Agatha.

"Mrs. Raisin, when did you last visit the Republic of Ireland?"

"What's that got to do with anything?"

"Please just answer the question," he rapped out.

Despite his unremarkable appearance, there was something menacing about Fother.

"I haven't," said Agatha. "I mean, I never got around to going there. On holidays, you know, I think of sun."

"And Northern Ireland?"

"Never been there either."

"We can check."

"Oh, please do," said Agatha, her temper beginning to rise.

"Have you heard of a man called Johnny Mulligan?"

"No. Who is he?"

"He is the dead gentleman on your kitchen floor. He was a foot soldier with the Provisional IRA. He was in the Maze Prison for murder but released under Tony Blair's famous amnesty."

"Could he have got the wrong house?" asked Charles. "I mean, Agatha's got nothing to do with anywhere in Ireland or politics."

"We'll get to you later, Sir Charles. In the meantime, it would be helpful if you would remain silent."

Fother fastened his gaze on Agatha again. "Mulligan was killed by some sort of poison. There was an empty coffee-cup on the table. The contents are being analysed, as is the jar of coffee. So far, we know the jar of coffee did not have any prints on it, which looks as if someone doctored it with poison. Perhaps someone who expected a visit from him?"

"I used the coffee I left in the kitchen before I left for Paris. I had a cup of it. Are you feeling well, Charles? You've gone rather white."

"What if," said Charles, "someone not connected at all decided to try to poison Agatha and whoever this Mulligan was drank it instead?"

"Who, for instance?"

Should I tell them about Emma? wondered Charles desperately. It would be awful if she turned out to be completely innocent. He rallied, "Maybe someone from one of Agatha's cases."

"Police are going through her files at the moment. You look upset. Are you sure you have no idea who put the poison there?"

"No idea," said Charles.

Fother turned back to Agatha. "Why did you go to Paris?"

"I felt like a break," said Agatha, "and Charles wanted to look up a friend's daughter who works at the couture house Thierry Duval. Her name is Felicity Felliet. We were told she was on holiday but due back the next day."

"And you decided to sacrifice the price of two plane tickets just to wait and see this girl?"

"Not really. As we were in Paris, we thought it might be a good idea to double-check Mr. Laggat-Brown's alibi. Mrs. Laggat-Brown hired me to work on the attempted shooting of her daughter."

"We'll leave that for the moment." Fother clasped his large hands together and leaned forward. "Before he turned terrorist, Mulligan was an expert burglar. It was said he could get in anywhere. Yet the pane of glass on the kitchen door was smashed by a rock. If you had been at home, you would have heard the noise, believe me.

"That makes me think again about Sir Charles's idea. We may have two people here. One wants to poison you and the other to shoot you. Perhaps the poisoner came back to see if he had left anything incriminating and finds the dead body. Panics and wants it to look like a break-in. Takes the poisoned coffee away and replaces it with a new jar, wiping it for fingerprints first. Now, Doris

Simpson had the keys to your house. The fact that the burglar alarm did not go off when Mulligan got in looks as if it was not on at all but was reset later."

"Doris would never do anything to hurt me!" exclaimed Agatha.

"We'll see. She is making a statement at this moment."

There was a tap at the door. Bill Wong's head appeared around it. "A word with you, sir."

Wilkes, who was sitting next to Fother, made as if to rise, but Fother stood up and went out of the room.

"I wish, Mrs. Raisin," said Wilkes, "that you would behave like the retired lady you're supposed to be."

"The tape's still running," said Charles.

Wilkes rose to switch it off but sat down again as Fother came back into the room.

"Doris Simpson says in her statement that a Mrs. Emma Comfrey, who works for you and lives next door to you, asked her for your keys, saying it would save Doris the trouble of coming and going to look after your cats. Then Mrs. Simpson changed her mind and demanded the keys back, saying that as you were paying her for the work, she would feel she was cheating you if she did not do it herself. What have you to say to that?"

But Fother turned his gaze on Charles, not Agatha.

"Sir Charles? I believe you think you know who might have tried to poison Mrs. Raisin."

"I took Emma Comfrey out for lunch a couple of times," said Charles in a flat voice. "I think she got a crush on me. She had started stalking me. I think she may have been jealous of my friendship with Agatha. And yet I find it hard to believe she would have gone to such lengths."

"We'll see. We're bringing her in. I will question her myself. Now we will begin at the beginning again. Your exact movements, Mrs. Raisin, starting with your journey to Paris."

Emma sat in the back of the police car, her mind going round and round. At times she felt her very brain was spinning with fear in her head.

She was sure they couldn't have found out anything. Then she realized that Doris must have told them about her having the keys. Well, she thought breathlessly, she would simply say that she had not gone in before Doris had claimed the keys back again. She must keep her nerve. She had worked long years for the Ministry of Defence. She was a respectable woman. No one could believe her capable of attempted murder.

The day had turned chilly and grey. The long Indian summer was over and the leaves were turning red, brown and gold.

She expected to be interviewed by Bill Wong, who had taken her initial statement.

Emma was led to an interviewing room. Courage, she told herself. You survived the Superglue investigation. You'll survive this one.

It was not Bill Wong who entered, but the men who had broken off interviewing Agatha and Charles to see what they could get out of her.

She paled slightly when Fother introduced himself. It must be serious. What was someone from the Special Branch doing in Mircester?

The tape was switched on and Fother began. "You are Mrs. Emma Comfrey. You live in Lilac Lane next door to Mrs. Agatha Raisin."

"That is so," said Emma, feeling a great calmness descending on her now that the interview had begun.

"Lilac Lane is a dead end and there are only the two cottages in it."

"Yes."

"Now, you went to Mrs. Raisin's cleaner and asked for the keys to Mrs. Raisin's cottage. Why?"

"I thought I would save her the time by looking after Agatha's cats myself."

"You are employed by Mrs. Raisin's detective agency. Why weren't you at work?"

"I had been working very hard and decided to take a day off."

"But you had also taken the previous day off to go to the fête at Barfield House."

Emma's calm deserted her. "I did not," she said in a trembling voice.

"According to both Sir Charles and his manservant, Gustav, you were seen there. The manservant was disguised as Madame Zora. You consulted him."

"Oh, I should have been working, I know," said Emma, rallying all her forces, although she was reeling inside from the shock that Gustav had been Madame Zora. "But Charles and I are friends and I happened to be in the area looking for . . . for a lost dog. The day was fine after the rain. Charles had told me about the fête."

"Yet you did not approach him."

"He was very busy. I stayed for a little and then went back to work."

"It is Sir Charles's opinion that you were stalking him."

Emma suddenly did not care any more what happened to

her. "That's ridiculous," she expostulated. "The vanity of men never fails to surprise me. You make a friendly gesture and they all think you are chasing them."

"We'll leave that for a moment." Fother leaned across the table towards her. "So when exactly did you enter Mrs. Raisin's cottage?"

"I didn't," protested Emma. "I did not have time. Doris claimed the keys back before I had time."

"Had you seen the dead man before? You joined Mrs. Simpson while she was waiting for the police."

"No, never."

"When were you last in Ireland?"

"Fourteen years ago. On holiday. We went to Cork."

The questioning went on and on while Charles and Agatha waited nervously in the adjoining room.

"This is serious, Aggie," Charles was saying. "That dead man in your kitchen was connected to the Provisional IRA. He was a hit man. Someone wanted you out of the picture."

"I can't stop thinking about Emma." Agatha ran her fingers through her hair. "I mean, do you think she might have tried to poison me?"

"I tried to warn you. There's something not right about her."

"If she's used rat poison, they'll find traces of it somewhere. Where would she hide it? In her garden?"

"I would think she'd want to get it out of her house and garden and as far away as possible. If it were me, I'd dump it in the woods somewhere—you know, in the undergrowth.

"Anyway," Charles went on, "what on earth can the Irish connection be? Was Peterson working for them in some capacity, bagman or something?"

"In that case you would think the terrorists would be after whoever killed him."

After an hour and several cups of bad coffee supplied by a policewoman, their interrogators came back.

Detective Inspector Wilkes took over the interview. When the tape was switched on, he said, "Mrs. Raisin, were you aware that your phone was being bugged?"

"No!" Agatha's eyes widened in shock.

"I want you to tell us all you know about the shooting at the Laggat-Browns."

Agatha marshalled the facts, leaving out the all-important one that Patrick Mullen had phoned her to tell her where Harrison Peterson was staying and that he wanted to talk.

Questions, and more questions. The day wore on. At last Fother said, "We have arranged a safe house for you, Mrs. Raisin. I suggest, also, that you do not go to your detective agency for the next few days. Sir Charles, I suggest you stay in the safe house with Mrs. Raisin for your own protection. We will call on you tomorrow for further questioning. Before you leave, we would like to check your mobile phones to make sure they are secure. Then tell us what clothes you want us to collect for you."

While they waited for their phones to be checked, Agatha thought again about Emma. Just to be on the safe side, she'd better phone her solicitor and get that codicil taken out.

Mrs. Bloxby had endured an exhausting day. Angry villagers kept calling at the vicarage, wanting Agatha Raisin expelled from the village. Somehow it had got out about the would-be killer having had a gun and a Balaclava. By setting up as a detective agency, Agatha Raisin had brought terror to Carsely, they said.

The vicar's wife answered each as patiently as she could, pointing out that several murderers would still be roaming free if it hadn't been for the work of Mrs. Raisin. At last she told her husband that she was not going to answer the door that evening. She poured herself a rare glass of sherry and took it out to the garden. She was just sitting down at the garden table with her drink when the doorbell went again. Ignoring its shrill summons, she sipped her sherry and watched the light fading over the churchyard at the end of the garden.

And then a plaintive voice from the churchyard hailed her. "Mrs. Bloxby!"

"Who's there?" she demanded sharply.

"It's me, Emma Comfrey. I must talk to you."

Mrs. Bloxby sighed. "Come round to the door."

When she let Emma in, she thought the woman looked on the edge of a breakdown. Her eyes were red with weeping and her hands trembled.

"Come into the garden," said Mrs. Bloxby. "Would you like a sherry?"

"No, thank you. I've just got to talk to someone."

No sooner were they seated than Emma burst out with "They think I tried to poison Agatha!"

"Did you?" asked Mrs. Bloxby quietly.

"Of course not. I wouldn't dream . . . Oh, it's worse than that."

"I can't think of anything worse. Go on."

"Charles told the police I had been stalking him."

"And had you?"

"No, I hadn't!" shouted Emma. And then, quietly, "It's all a dreadful mistake. I went to the fête at Barfield House, that's all."

"Why did you go there when you should have been working?"

"I was working in the area. Charles is . . . was . . . a friend of mine."

"What did he say when you saw him?"

"I didn't approach him because he was so busy."

"If there is nothing in it," said Mrs. Bloxby, "then you have nothing to worry about. All you need to do is to keep well clear of Sir Charles Fraith in future."

"But don't you see, I have to talk to him. I have to ask him why he said such a dreadful thing. I was interrogated for hours."

The doorbell shrilled again. "I'd better answer that." Mrs. Bloxby was suddenly anxious not to be alone with Emma.

She opened the door.

"Police," said a plainclothes officer. "The forensic team have finished with Mrs. Raisin's cottage for the moment and would like to go into Mrs. Comfrey's cottage. Is she here?"

"Yes, I'll fetch her."

Mrs. Bloxby went back into the garden. "Mrs. Comfrey, a forensic team wishes to examine your cottage."

Emma turned pale. "Can't I just give them the keys and stay here?"

"I'm afraid not. But just let's hope nothing happens to Mrs. Raisin, because if it does, Mrs. Comfrey, I'm afraid you might find yourself the first suspect."

Emma clutched her arm. "You think I did it!"

Mrs. Bloxby pulled her arm away. "Please go, Mrs. Comfrey. I must get my husband's supper and the police are waiting for you."

*   *   *

"I always wondered what a safe house would look like," said Agatha. "Not much, is it? It's not a house anyway. It's a flat."

The flat was situated in a block on the outskirts of Mircester. The flats had been newly built and several were still vacant. Theirs was sparsely furnished with the bare essentials. There were three bedrooms: one for herself, one for Charles, and one for their minder, a burly individual in plainclothes who answered to the name of Terry.

Agatha went into the kitchen. There was milk in the fridge and teabags and a jar of instant coffee were on the counter.

"What about food?" asked Agatha.

"I've got list of food deliveries," said Terry. "Tell me what you want and I'll phone for it. There's Indian, Chinese, pizza— you name it."

"What about drink?" asked Charles. "I could do with a stiff one."

"I can get the local supermarket to deliver. They're open twenty-four hours."

"I'll give you a shopping list," said Agatha, "because we'll need stuff for breakfast as well."

When Terry was on the phone, Charles drew Agatha aside and whispered, "Say we're going to share a bedroom."

"Honestly, Charles, at such a time!"

"Pillow talk. We need to talk and we can't do it with him listening."

"Okay."

After they had eaten and watched several programmes on television, Charles said he and Agatha were going to bed.

Terry said he thought it would be better if he slept on the sofa, "just to be on the safe side." He added the caution, "Don't go using your mobiles and telling anyone at all where you are."

Once Agatha and Charles were in bed, he snuggled up to her. "Get off!" whispered Agatha fiercely.

"We've got to talk," he whispered. "Let's start with Emma. Let's just suppose she tried to poison you. She'd be clever enough to get rid of the stuff. Where would she put it? Where would you put it?"

"Same idea as you . . . in the woods somewhere."

"She'd be frightened of anyone seeing her, maybe meeting a gamekeeper. The woods around are criss-crossed with paths for ramblers and people walking their dogs. Think again."

"There's something at the back of my mind," said Agatha slowly. "I know. It was one day in the office. Emma said there was some rubbish in the shed at the bottom of the garden she wanted rid of. A broken chair, a table with one leg missing, that sort of thing. Miss Simms said, 'Why don't you take the lot out to the council tip on the old Worcester Road,' and gave her directions. As soon as we get out of here, let's go and have a look."

"I wonder how long they mean to keep us here?" said Charles.

"God knows. It's going to be like being in prison. There must be some connection between the hit man and the killing of Peterson."

"Wait a bit," said Charles. "Wasn't there something you said about Laggat-Brown changing his name from Ryan? Ryan's an Irish name."

"It can't be him," said Agatha impatiently. "He's a charming and civilized man. Besides, he can't have had anything to do with the attempted shooting. His own daughter, too! And we've double-checked his alibi."

"You've got a soft spot for him, Aggie."

"Well, he took me out for dinner and he paid the bill, which is more than you ever do."

They grumbled and discussed the case and grumbled again until they both fell asleep.

Terry, who had pressed his ear against their bedroom door, quietly retreated and picked up the phone. He suggested the forensic team should check the council tip on the old Worcester Road.

Emma had moved into a hotel in Moreton-in-Marsh for the night. She tossed and turned, wondering whether she was safe or not.

She felt that she should check the council tip in the morning and try to find out when the containers were taken away. Until she knew that, she felt she could not rest.

The morning dawned cold and misty. The only colour in the bleached countryside was the red of the autumn leaves. She drove steadily and carefully, although her hands on the steering wheel were damp with nerves.

She turned off the old Worcester Road and headed for the tip. She was just about to turn in at the entrance when up ahead, through the swirling morning mist, she saw the white-coated figures of a forensic team.

Emma reversed slowly, and once out on the road, put her foot down on the accelerator and sped to the hotel.

She hurried to her room and packed up the few belongings she had taken for her overnight stay. She paid her bill and estimated she had a very short time before they found the coffee jar and the rat poison. She had not left fingerprints but knew that the very fact they were searching the tip meant they thought she was guilty.

Emma got in her car, wondering whether to risk going home

and collecting some more things, but then decided against it. She had arrangements to draw money on a bank in Moreton, but if she wanted to clean out her account she would need to go to the head bank in London. An hour and a half to London. She might just make it.

There was an agonizing wait at the bank while they dealt with her request to draw out twenty thousand pounds. When she at last got the money, she went to the nearest hairdresser and got her heavy hair cut to a short crop and dyed dark brown. Then she went into a shop and bought jeans, sweaters, T-shirts and an anorak and trainers. She changed into a new outfit in the fitting room, where she left the clothes from her suitcase and filled it with the new purchases. A shop assistant, finding the clothes later, did not think to report the find to the police. She took the clothes home to her mother.

Emma knew she needed a new car, one that would not be traced for some time. She abandoned the car in a side street and took a taxi to Victoria Station and put her suitcase in the "Left Luggage" and then took the tube to the East End.

She found a shady-looking car dealer and paid cash for a small Ford van, then drove into central London, leaving it near Victoria in an underground car-park. Emma had a frightening time at the station, hoping any police there would not recognize her. She had bought a rain hat in the East End and had the brim pulled well down to shadow her face.

She got back to the van and slung her suitcase in the back. Now where? At first she thought of driving north and into the wilds of Scotland, but she had read stories of people who did that and found they were more noticeable out in the Highland wilderness than they were in a town.

Scarborough, she thought. A seaside town which would still have a lot of end-of-season visitors. She drove steadily north out of London. By the time she reached Yorkshire, the van engine was making strange clanking sounds. She thought of abandoning it on the Yorkshire moors and then decided against it. The police would be called to any abandoned car. She drove instead into York and parked in a suburb. She took out her suitcases and left the keys in the van, hoping someone would steal it.

Emma then caught a bus to the railway station and took a train to Scarborough. She longed to take a taxi into town because she was beginning to feel weary, but decided, despite her altered appearance, that it would be safe to take the bus. She then found a small, anonymous-looking bed-and-breakfast and checked in.

Only when she was in a small dingy bedroom with the door shut and locked did she collapse on the bed and feel anger like poison bubbling up inside her. Charles had betrayed her. Charles had humiliated her. He had called her a stalker and he should suffer for it if it was the last thing she did.

It was decided after four days to release Agatha and Charles from the safe house. "It's not as if they're prime witnesses to appear in court," said Father, "and it's costing the state money."

"But someone might kill Mrs. Raisin," said Detective Inspector Wilkes, to which Father replied sourly, "Good. I can't stand amateurs."

Father went to the safe house to tell them they were now free to go about their business. "Emma Comfrey is still missing," he said. "We found rat poison and the jar of poisoned coffee at the council tip on the old Worcester Road."

Agatha glared at Terry. "You've been listening at doors."

"You underestimate the intelligence of the police," said Fother coldly. "I suggest, Mrs. Raisin, that in future you leave the Laggat-Brown case alone and concentrate on divorces and missing cats."

Agatha and Charles were driven in a police car to Agatha's house. Charles collected his own car. "I'm going home," he said to Agatha.

"Aren't you going to help me any more?" asked Agatha.

"I think we need a break from each other," said Charles coldly. "All you've done in the last few days is pick on me when they weren't interrogating us over and over again." Agatha had indeed taken her frustration at being cooped up out on Charles but would not even admit to herself that she was guilty of anything.

"Just like you," she snapped. "Selfish to the bone."

"You should know," retorted Charles, getting into his car. "You wrote the book on selfishness."

He drove off. The police car followed him. Agatha stood forlornly on her doorstep and watched them go. Then she put her key in the lock and went inside.

No cats came to greet her. She phoned Doris Simpson, who said, "I've got them. They've been playing with my cat, Scrabble. I'll bring them around. I didn't want to leave the poor things there. When the police were finished, I scrubbed everything clean."

"I'll give you a bonus," said Agatha. "See you soon."

She phoned the agency. Patrick Mullen answered the phone. "Don't worry about a thing," he said. "Everything's been running smoothly. There's no such thing as bad publicity and we've got as much work as we can handle. I took the liberty of getting a girl from a temp agency to answer the phones because your Miss

Simms is a dab hand at detecting. Got a natural bent for it. Are you coming in?"

"I'm waiting for my cats," said Agatha, "and then I'll be with you in about an hour."

When Doris arrived, Agatha, suddenly lonely, tried to get her to stay but Doris said she was working a shift at a supermarket in Evesham and couldn't wait.

Agatha sat on the kitchen floor and petted her cats. Then she rose and took some fish out of the freezer, defrosted it and cooked it for them. After they were fed, she patted them again and then left for Mircester.

When she entered the agency and saw Patrick sitting behind her desk she couldn't help thinking he looked like the real thing compared to herself.

"I need some lunch, Patrick," she said. "Join me and fill me in."

Patrick said he wanted sausage, bacon and eggs. Agatha, aware that the waistband of her skirt was uncomfortably tight after her days of inactivity in the safe house, opted for a salad.

"As far as I can gather, this Mulligan is known to Special Branch from the days he worked for the Provisional IRA. They are trying to figure out why he came after you. The only case you have, they say, which involved a shooting was the Laggat-Brown one."

"Laggat-Brown changed his name from Ryan," said Agatha. "Why?"

"The cynical cops think it was because he wanted to marry Mrs. Laggat-Brown and all that money from dog biscuits, and she didn't think his name was grand enough. But he seems to be squeaky-clean. He left the firm of stockbrokers he was working for with a clean bill of health. He runs an import/export agency selling electronic parts here and there. Mainly a one-man operation, but he was trained in electronics. He also got a first in physics from Cambridge University. Parents both dead. Lived in Dublin but moved with young Jeremy to England when he was fifteen. Mother, housewife; father, a plumber."

"A plumber! Can't have been much money in the family."

"Then you don't know much about plumbers. They can earn a mint."

"I had dinner with Jeremy Laggat-Brown. He was charming."

Patrick looked at her with his lugubrious eyes. "If he asks you out again, don't discuss the case with him."

"Why not? You say he's squeaky-clean."

"That's what the police say. But better to be careful. As to Harrison Peterson's death, it seems that he was given a massive dose of digitalis, not in the vodka but in some coffee. He had a dicky heart and that's what killed him. The pathologist who performed the first autopsy said he had missed the real cause of death because he was overworked and it looked from the police report like an open-and-shut case of suicide. They found traces of coffee in his stomach. They think when he passed out that the murderer heaved him onto the bed."

"So his murderer must have known about his medical condition?"

"Right. So take time off and forget about the Laggat-Browns for the moment."

Agatha gave a little sigh, thinking that an evening out with a handsome man like Jeremy Laggat-Brown was just what she needed. She suddenly wondered about Patrick. Did he have a wife? A family?

He was in his sixties, tall with stooped shoulders, oily brown hair and a faintly unkempt appearance.

"Are you married?" asked Agatha.

"I was. But my hours of work broke up the marriage."

"Children?"

"A son and a daughter, both married with children of their own. Let me fill you in on the business we've been doing while you were away." He crisply outlined new cases, what Miss Simms was following up and what Sammy Allen and Douglas Ballantine were doing.

Agatha began to feel superfluous. "I'd better start doing some work," she said.

"Why don't you take a couple of days off?" suggested Patrick. "But it would be better to leave the Laggat-Brown case alone until things cool down."

Agatha was about to protest. She took a mirror out of her handbag to repair her lipstick and noticed with dismay that she had an incipient moustache.

"Maybe just one day," she said.

She drove to Evesham and to the Beaumonde Beauty Salon where she secured the services of her favourite beautician, a pretty woman called Dawn. After her moustache had been removed and her eyebrows plucked, she indulged in a non-surgical facelift and emerged an hour and a half later feeling like a new woman.

She drove home and played with the cats and then remembered she hadn't checked her phone for messages.

There was one from Roy Silver, asking excitedly about the poisoning and then one from Jeremy Laggat-Brown, saying that he was worried about her and suggesting that they meet.

Roy could wait. She phoned the mobile phone number that Jeremy had given her.

His pleasant voice said, "Agatha! What about dinner?"

"What about your wife?"

"She's gone off with Jason to the funeral parlour. The body's being released. What if I pick you up in half an hour?"

"Can you make it an hour? I need a shower."

When she had rung off, Agatha leaped up the stairs, noticing there was that twinge in her hip again. Probably strained it, she thought. She had a quick shower and chose a simple black wool dress and black court shoes. That, with a light coat, would not make her look so overdressed as she had been last time.

Emma was sitting at the moment in a pub in Scarborough working her way through an enormous steak pie and chips. She was deliberately putting on weight and noticed with satisfaction that her face was already fatter and that, combined with her cropped hair, made her look very different from the Emma Comfrey the police were looking for.

There was little to do with her days but eat large meals, change her boarding-house, and walk along the promenade watching the surging waves and plotting revenge.

Her hate focused on Charles Fraith, who had deliberately led her on, only to betray her. It was because of him that she was on the run. The fact that she had tried to poison Agatha Raisin did not cause her one pang of guilt. It was all Charles's fault. She had seen her photograph flashed up on the television news programmes, but it was an old one from her Ministry of Defence days and she knew that her new appearance bore no resemblance to the face on the screen. She also deliberately "commonized" her accent, adopting the singsong tones of Birmingham.

In the past two days, her name and photograph had disappeared from the newspapers. A few more days, and she might make her way south when she had formulated a plan about what to do to Charles.

NINE

✝

AGATHA did not enjoy the dinner as much as she had expected. She found she was worrying about Charles.

In her working days in London, she had been friendless. Her public relations firm was successful and consumed all her energies. Since moving to Carsely, Bill Wong had been her first friend, and then Mrs. Bloxby and Charles. She realized with a guilty pang that she had always taken Charles for granted. He came and went, often staying with her for quite long periods of time. She worried more about the emotional welfare of her cats than she did of that of Charles.

"You haven't told me how you're progressing with the case," said Jeremy. "I've asked you twice, but you were staring off into space and not listening. There seems to have been a black-out on it in the newspapers. They only published that a murdered man had been found in your kitchen but nothing about who he was."

"I'm sorry," said Agatha. "I'm a bit distracted at the moment. I really must phone your wife. I have been instructed by the police and Special Branch to leave the case alone for the moment."

"Special Branch? Why them?"

He smiled into her eyes, but Agatha remembered Patrick's warning and so she lied. "They wouldn't tell me."

"And where were you for the last few days? I called several times."

"I stayed at some hotel with Charles. I didn't want to go home while the house was crawling with forensic people. Then the press usually come round in swarms."

"So you don't know who the man was?"

"No."

"You'd never seen him before?" His eyes teased her. "Not a rejected lover, hey?"

Agatha smiled. "Nothing like that." What was Charles doing? Had she been so very rude to him? "Bugger rocket," she said, poking at the green mound on her plate.

He looked startled.

"Sorry," said Agatha. "I didn't realize I had spoken aloud. Rocket's not my favourite vegetable."

"I heard you were in Paris when the murder took place. What took you there?"

"I needed a break and Charles wanted to look up an old friend's daughter."

"What's her name?"

Agatha began to feel a tinge of unease. "I don't know because we never saw her. The police hauled us in and that was that. Never mind the dreadful murder. Let's talk about something else. Are you going to the funeral?"

"No, I've got to work. Might be away for a bit."

"Are you reconciled with your wife?"

"Pretty much. But only for Cassandra's sake. She wants us to be together. But it'll be a marriage in name only." He smiled at her again. "We'll be able to see a lot of each other."

"I don't date men if their living with their exes," said Agatha. He laughed. "You are now."

"But that's different. You're part of a case I'm working on."

"I thought you weren't working on it."

"As I said, not at the moment. And you are the ex-husband of a client."

He took her hand. "And is that all?"

He was extremely handsome and possibly, if she had not been worrying about the absent Charles, she might have succumbed to his charm. But she drew her hand away gently and said, "I'm not in the mood for a flirtation at the moment, Jeremy. This murder and all has frightened me out of my wits. You do see that."

"Of course, of course." He began to talk about other things and then drove her home.

Agatha said goodbye to him on the doorstep. He tried to kiss her on the lips, but she turned her face so that the kiss fell on her cheek.

Once inside, she decided to phone Roy.

"You seem to be having a hairy time, sweetie," he said. "Want me to come down?"

"Oh, would you?" Agatha was suddenly flooded with gratitude.

"I've got a few days owing. I'll be down tomorrow. There's a train gets in at Moreton around twelve-thirty."

"I'll be there."

Agatha then phoned Charles's number. Gustav answered the phone. "Who's calling?" he asked in reply to her demand to speak to Charles.

"Agatha Raisin."

Gustav promptly rang off and Agatha gazed at the phone in a fury.

She was just about to turn away when the phone rang. Agatha answered it with a cautious "Yes."

"It's Mrs. Bloxby here. Someone in the village said you were back. Are you on your own or is Charles there?"

"I'm on my own. Charles has left."

"I think I should pack a bag and spend the night with you."

Agatha was just opening her mouth to say that would be wonderful when she heard the vicar's voice grumbling in the background, "Honestly, Margaret, you're running yourself ragged. That Raisin female is old enough to look after herself."

"Wait a minute," said Mrs. Bloxby. She covered the receiver with her hand, but Agatha could hear faint sounds of an altercation.

When Mrs. Bloxby came back on the phone, Agatha said hurriedly, "I'm really all right. Honestly. Roy's coming tomorrow to stay."

"If you're sure . . ."

"Absolutely."

The day before, the owner of the Sea View bed-and-breakfast—a view of the sea was only possible if one walked one hundred yards down the road—was becoming nervous about one of her guests.

This Mrs. Elder was a good customer and paid cash, but she had begun to talk to herself—not out loud, but her lips were constantly moving and her eyes glaring. The owner, Mrs. Blythe, was a widow and wished she had a man around to advise her. The holiday season was over and she had to rely on weekend visitors.

Emma, who had adopted the name of Mrs. Elder, had been in the television room. She passed Mrs. Blythe in the hall, her eyes glazed and her lips moving. Mrs. Blythe made up her mind. "Mrs. Elder!" she said sharply.

Emma started and focused on her.

"I'm sorry this is such short notice, but I'll be needing your room."

Emma stared at her for a long time. Mrs. Blythe expected her to protest, but Emma decided this was The Sign she had been waiting for. Time to go south.

"Thank you," she said mildly. "I shall leave after breakfast."

Mrs. Blythe watched her visitor mount the stairs. Why, Mrs. Elder had sounded quite normal.

Agatha was glad when morning dawned. She had drifted in and out of an uneasy sleep. The trouble with old thatched cottages was that beams creep and things rustle in the thatch. The first winds of autumn had risen during the night and the lilac tree in the front garden scraped its branches against the window.

She went down to the general stores as soon as they opened to buy treats for her cats. There were several other people in the shop and the atmosphere was frosty. Agatha was still being blamed by the villagers for having brought in violence from that outside world of murder and mayhem.

But Agatha was too worried and edgy to notice the atmosphere. She bought pâté and cream and frozen fish for the cats, went home and fed them, and drove to her office in Mircester. The wind was sending leaves skittering across the road in front of her car. Autumn was the only time when Agatha missed London. One didn't notice the seasons much in the city. But in autumn in the country, you could practically feel everything dying and became aware of your own mortality.

In the office, Patrick seemed to have everything in hand. Agatha decided to visit Harrison Peterson's former wife, Joyce, again. Her new partner was obviously capable of violence.

Thoughts of Emma still at large floated uneasily through Agatha's mind. But she wouldn't dare try again. Would she?

The autumn mist of earlier that morning had lifted and a small white sun shone down over the brown ploughed fields.

Agatha drove steadily along the Fosseway, her eyes flicking occasionally to the speed dial because the police with speed cameras had started using unmarked vehicles.

She turned off on the road down into Shipston-on-Stour and drove into the car-park opposite Joyce Peterson's house. Agatha found the last parking place available with a feeling of triumph because a car which came in after her had to circle round and round, waiting for someone to leave.

She did not know that PC Betty Howse was in that car, having been ordered to tail Agatha.

Agatha walked across the road and rang the bell. There was a long silence. She rang the bell again.

At last, Joyce Peterson opened the door. She had been crying. Her beautiful face was blotched with tears.

"I wondered how you were doing," Agatha began.

Joyce looked nervously over her shoulder. "Now is not a good time to call," she said. "I'm busy."

She was suddenly jerked aside and Mark loomed in the

doorway. "You!" he said in accents of loathing. He towered over Agatha, who backed out onto the pavement. Mark followed her.

Agatha was wearing a loose silk blouse under her open coat. He seized her blouse by the neck and twisted it and then banged her up against the wall of the cottage.

"You leave us alone, you old bitch," he raged. He gave Agatha's head a nasty thump against the wall.

A cool voice behind them said, "Let her go immediately."

Betty Howse was in plainclothes.

"Get lost." Mark banged Agatha's head again.

"That's it," said Betty. She flashed her warrant card. "Mark Goddham, I am charging you with assault." She recited the caution while Mark stood frozen.

Agatha had read in books of people's eyes going red with fury and thought the description poetic licence, but Mark's eyes did look red as they blazed with anger.

He released Agatha and stared down at Betty.

"And just how are you going to take me in?"

He reached out to grab Betty, who produced one of those expanding police batons from behind her back and whacked him over the legs. As he doubled up, she twisted him round and handcuffed him.

"You wait there," she said to Agatha. She radioed for assistance.

"You are charging him with assault, aren't you?" Betty said to Agatha.

"Definitely."

The change in Mark was almost ludicrous. The fury had all gone out of him and he stood there with his head hanging.

"Look, we can sort this out," he pleaded. "It was all a mistake."

"I'll just see if Joyce is all right." Agatha walked into the house.

Joyce was sitting on a sofa, rocking backwards and forwards, her face now twisted with pain.

"I think he broke my ribs," she whispered.

Agatha left her and went out again. "Joyce Peterson needs an ambulance."

Betty spoke into her radio. "Is she bad?" she asked Agatha.

"She thinks her ribs are broken."

"Keep her company until the ambulance arrives," said Betty, "and I'll watch this bastard here."

Agatha went back inside. "Would you like a cup of tea?" she asked.

Joyce shook her head. "I'm charging him with assault, so you may as well do the same thing," said Agatha.

There came the sounds of a scuffle outside, then they heard Mark crying out in pain, and Betty's voice calmly charging him with assaulting a police officer.

"There you are," said Agatha. "Two charges of assault. You'd better make it a third."

"Will he go to prison?"

"Of course."

She gave a broken little sob. "Then I will charge him as well. May I have some brandy, please? There's a bottle over there with the other drinks."

Agatha reflected that hot sweet tea would be a better idea, but decided that she could do with a brandy herself. She poured two stiff measures and carried them over.

Joyce took a gulp and shuddered. "You never can tell with men," she said. "I thought he was God's gift to women when I met him. He was so charming, so attentive. It was just after he moved in with me that the beatings started. He always cried afterwards and begged my forgiveness, but he would always start again after a few days."

"What caused this latest assault?"

"I said I wanted to go to Harrison's funeral, that's all it took."

"Were you fond of Harrison?"

"For quite a time. Then he started travelling a lot and he was hardly ever home. When he was sent to prison, I was so angry with him that I wanted to get a divorce and make a clear break. Jason was devoted to his father. I don't think he ever forgave me. When I was invited to the Laggat-Browns' party, Mark wouldn't let me go."

Sirens were sounding outside as both police and ambulance arrived. Joyce was examined and helped out to the ambulance. Agatha watched and was photographed for the local paper. The whole of Shipston-on-Stour seemed to be crowding into the street to watch.

Mark Goddham was thrust into a police car. Agatha found herself facing Bill Wong.

"You'd better follow me back to Mircester," said Bill, "and give me a statement. Are you fit to drive?"

Agatha felt the back of her head, which was sore and tender. "I feel a bit shaky. He really did bang my head against that wall. Oh, Lord!" She glanced at her watch. "I'm supposed to pick Roy up at Moreton."

"You'd better leave your car and come with me. We can swing round by the railway station and pick up Roy."

*   *   *

At Agatha's insistence, Bill, who was driving a police car, turned on the siren and broke the speed limit along the Fosseway and into the station yard just as the passengers were alighting from the London train.

Agatha called to Roy and he slid into the back of the police car, his eyes gleaming with excitement.

"What's going on?" he asked.

"Agatha's been assaulted," said Bill. "We're taking her into police headquarters to make a statement."

"Are you all right?" asked Roy. "Who assaulted you?"

Agatha told him her story and then burst into tears. Bill handed her a box of tissues and said, "I'll get a doctor to examine you, Agatha. I don't think I've ever known you to cry before."

Emma had zigzagged down towards Warwickshire, taking country buses although she felt that no policeman would recognize her now with her new clothes, cropped hair and the extra weight she had put on.

She had bought a hunting knife and put it in the bottom of her capacious handbag. The thought of that sharp steel nestling there warmed her heart. She left her last bus in Stratford-on-Avon and set out to walk the long miles to Barfield House.

Charles would have gone back to see Agatha because he never held on to resentments for very long. But he had fallen for a leggy brunette called Elaine Wisbich who worked for the Countryside Alliance and had come calling to ask for a contribution. He had taken her out for dinner on the previous day and was meeting her again for lunch in Stratford.

She was already waiting in the restaurant when Charles arrived. Elaine had masses of thick brown curly hair. Her face was long and very white with a small mouth. Her eyes were disproportionately small. But she had a generous bust and those long, long legs.

The meal went pleasantly, although Charles wished she wouldn't laugh so much since she had a high, braying, ugly laugh. He lit a cigarette at the end of the meal and she playfully said, "Naughty, naughty," and took it out of his mouth and ground it out in the ashtray.

Charles sighed as love died. When he called for the bill, he found to his dismay that he really had left his wallet this time. Charles was mean and occasionally pretended to have forgotten his wallet, but this time hc had meant to pay.

"I'm awfully sorry, Elaine," he said. "I've forgotten my wallet. If you pay, I'll pay you back."

Elaine had a voice like one of Bertie Wooster's aunts, which could be heard across a six-acre field, two spinneys and a paddock. That voice now sounded across the restaurant.

"You've cost me more than this lunch," said Elaine. "Alice Forbes bet me a tenner that you would try to get me to pay, but naïve little me said, 'Oh, no, Charles is a gentleman.'"

"I promise you, Elaine . . ."

"Forget it."

Elaine paid in furious silence and they separated outside the restaurant.

Charles drove to Barfield House, reflecting that he had the

farm account books to wrestle with, so he might as well get on with it. Charles never used the front door, which had a massive Victorian key to unlock it, and was about to go round the back when he saw the door was standing open.

I'll have a word with Gustav about that, thought Charles. In this day of seriously militant ramblers and New Age travellers, it was as well to keep doors locked at all times.

He paused for a moment in the hall and then went through to his study. He froze on the threshold, rigid with shock. His elderly aunt was bound to a chair and gagged.

Turning to face him with a long hunting knife in her hand was a woman he did not at first recognize. She was tall and heavy-set with brown cropped hair. But it was when she smiled that he recognized those teeth.

"Emma," he said. "What have you done to my aunt?"

"I've come to kill you."

"Why?" asked Charles, affecting a calmness he was far from feeling.

"Because you betrayed me."

"How on earth did I do that?"

"You told the police I was stalking you and yet it was you who led me on. Kneel before me and beg my forgiveness." The knife waved in the air.

She's gone really bonkers now, thought Charles, but he said in his usual pleasant light voice, "Don't be silly, Emma. Untie my aunt. You'll give her a heart attack."

"Kneel!" howled Emma.

Charles knelt down and shuffled forwards on his knees. "Don't hurt me," he begged.

Emma smiled. "Now that's better."

Charles lunged forward and grabbed her round the knees and sent her tumbling to the floor. The knife flew out of her grasp. She clawed and fought desperately.

Gustav walked into the room and, leaning down, grabbed Emma by the back of her coat and dragged her upright. Then he gave her two powerful slaps across the face.

Emma burst into tears. Gustav saw the bag she had brought with thin rope in it and took some rope out and tied her wrists and ankles.

He made to pick up the hunting knife to free the aunt's bonds, but Charles shouted, "Leave that, Gustav. We need the evidence."

Gustav nodded and went out and returned with a pair of kitchen scissors and proceeded to release the aunt, Mrs. Tassey. When she could speak, Mrs. Tassey said, "What a horrible woman. Gustav, call the police."

"Already being done," said Gustav, nodding to where Charles was speaking urgently on the phone.

Emma had slumped onto the floor and was curled up in the foetal position, rocking and crooning.

Charles had a great feeling of relief when he heard the approaching police sirens. He felt more relief when Emma was cautioned and taken off. He could only marvel at the resilience of his elderly aunt, who was drinking a large gin and tonic and making her statement. Emma had called and brandished the knife in Mrs. Tassey's face and had forced her to the study, where she had tied her up and gagged her.

At last their statements were all taken. Mrs. Tassey said she would do some gardening because that always soothed her and Charles decided it was time he went through the accounts. The phone rang. Gustav answered it.

"It's a Miss Wisbich," he said.

"I'd better take it," groaned Charles. "Hullo, Elaine. Terrible drama here." He told her of the attack by Emma.

"Gosh," said Elaine. "I mean, jolly exciting stuff. Did you really forget your wallet?"

"Really, honestly, definitely."

"You can make it up to me. There's a new French restaurant in Broadway called Cordon Bleu. You can take me there for dinner tomorrow night. It's *very* expensive."

"Oh, all right," said Charles. "Eight o'clock fine?"

"Great, see you there."

Agatha now had a policeman on guard outside her door. Bill Wong had tried to get her a police guard before, but Agatha's exploits caused such resentment at Mircester Police Headquarters that they had refused before, no doubt hoping, Bill thought, that someone really would get rid of her. PC Betty Howse had been instructed to tail her, not for Agatha's protection but to find out what she was up to.

Agatha had a large lump on the back of her head, but the skin had not been broken.

PC Darren Boyd, on guard outside her door, was a very good-looking young man. At first he had protested at the boring job, but now he was beginning to enjoy himself as the ladies of the village plied him with tea and cakes and hot sausage rolls. One even produced a garden chair for him to sit on, and another, a little table. Another brought him books and magazines. So he sat in the sun and passed a pleasant afternoon and was quite disappointed when his relief arrived.

Agatha was glad of the police presence to keep the press at bay. At first she could not understand why so many press were besieging her over a simple assault. It was only when she turned on the evening news and heard of Emma's attempt on Charles's life that she understood the reason for the fuss. Her name had been linked with Charles's on previous cases and Emma had tried to poison her.

She phoned Charles, but Gustav hung up on her.

"This is ridiculous," fumed Agatha. "He should sack that man."

"Let's go out there," suggested Roy.

"No good. Gustav will answer the door and then slam it in our faces. And the press will be all over the place."

Agatha's mobile rang. "I'd better answer it. Maybe the press haven't got this number."

"It's on your business cards," said Roy.

Nonetheless, Agatha picked up her mobile phone. "Agatha," said a warm deep voice. "It's me, Jeremy. I've just heard on the news that that woman who used to work for you has been arrested."

"I just heard it on the news. It is a relief. How are you getting on?"

"Oh, so-so. The commuting up and down to London's getting a bit wearing. I'm thinking of getting a small flat there and only coming down at the weekends. Jason's mourning his father, and life here is pretty dreary. Feel like having dinner with me tomorrow night?"

"I've got a guest staying, Roy Silver, who used to work for

me." There was a silence and then he said, "Bring him along as well. Is he amusing?"

"Yes, very."

"Just what I need. I'll see you both at eight."

"He's not interested in you romantically," said Roy when Agatha told him, "or he would never have included me in the invitation. He wants to pump you for information."

"Nonsense. The police have checked on him thoroughly. He's got a cast-iron alibi. And he tried to kiss me."

"We'll see."

TEN

†

AGATHA had forgotten that Roy Silver only dressed conventionally when he was working for some of his stuffier clients. So she was taken aback when he appeared in her living room, ready to go out, dressed in a black-and-white horizontally striped T-shirt and tight-fitting black trousers and with a red scarf knotted at his neck.

"Are you going like that?" she asked.

"What's up with it? You said we were going to a French restaurant, so I'm looking French."

"It's a comic-book idea of a Frenchman. What do you wear when you're going to a Chinese restaurant? A lampshade hat and a pigtail? Oh, come on, then. We're going to be late."

"What's the food like at this place?" asked Roy as he slid into the passenger seat. He had added a long black cloak to his ensemble. How did he get all that into a travel bag? wondered Agatha.

"Not very good," she said, letting in the clutch. "Don't order the duck. It's like rubber. And forget ordering a salad. It's mostly rocket."

"I like rocket."

"Then you'll be all right. It comes with everything."

"You're all glammed up," said Roy. "If the neckline of that dress was any lower, the police would have you for indecent exposure."

"I am perfectly respectable," protested Agatha, but before they got out of the car, she gave her neckline a surreptitious hitch upwards.

Jeremy was already there. An amused smile twitched his lips when he saw Roy. Agatha was just sitting down when she spotted Charles and a girl with a lot of brown curly hair sitting at a table at the other side of the restaurant.

"Good heavens," said Charles. "It's Agatha."

"Agatha who?" asked Elaine. "You mean the old bird flashing her boobs?"

"She's not that much older than me," said Charles defensively. "Let's go over and say hullo."

"Must we?"

"Only take a minute."

They walked over and Charles made the introductions. Agatha introduced Jeremy. "Where have you been, Charles?" asked Agatha in what Elaine thought was a proprietorial tone.

Elaine put her arm through Charles's. "I've been keeping him busy." And she let out her great braying laugh while Charles flinched.

"I'll be over tomorrow," said Charles. "We'll catch up on things then. Will you be in the office?"

"Yes, from nine o'clock on."

"See you then. Goodbye, Jeremy. Nice to meet you." And then Charles said something in rapid French.

Jeremy smiled and nodded.

"What did he say?" asked Agatha.

"Blessed if I know. His French is atrocious. Now, what would you like to eat?"

Roy had no appreciation of good food and so he enjoyed the meal simply because the ambience pleased him: the candle-light, the attentive waiters, and the very high prices.

Jeremy began to ask about how Agatha was proceeding with the case and had the police found out the identity of the dead man. Agatha lied and shook her head and lied again. But she did tell him about the arrest of Mark Goddham, knowing it would be in the papers in the morning. Then she added on impulse, "I can't talk about the case, Jeremy, really. The police have asked me not to. But I can tell you, I think I'm near a solution."

Roy chattered about his work in London and told several amusing stories. Occasionally they could hear the bray of Elaine's laughter sounding across the room. "Would you listen to her," complained Roy. "What's she eating? Oats?"

Agatha felt that twinge at her hip again as she rose from the table. She felt suddenly old. Elaine might have a dreadful laugh, but she was young. What if Charles married her? What would happen when she got older and the few friends she had faded away?

Outside the restaurant, Jeremy said to Roy, "You obviously know Agatha well."

Roy smirked. "We're terribly close," he said.

Jeremy laughed. "Oh, Agatha, and I thought that stunning dress was all for me."

"Roy is just a friend," snapped Agatha. She was furious with Roy. What if Jeremy's attempt at a new relationship with his ex-wife didn't work out? He was divorced and available.

"What came over you, Roy?" she demanded as she drove off. "Implying we had a relationship."

"Just protecting you, sweetie. I didn't like him and you say he's trying to repair his old marriage. So what's he doing romancing you?"

"I thought you said he was only interested in finding out information."

"Changed my mind. The way he looked at you! Like a wolf."

Agatha felt a little glow inside.

"And what were you about telling him you were near solving the case? He may be attracted to you, but if he's the real villain, it won't stop him having another go at you. And there's a car following us. It was behind us when we left Carsely and it's there again."

"Probably that woman PC who followed me to Joyce Peterson's. The police are keeping an eye on me."

They said good night to the policeman on duty outside Agatha's cottage.

"How long will they keep up the protection?" asked Roy.

Agatha sighed. "Not very long. Ever since this government closed down all the village police stations, Mircester find themselves overstretched. Fred Griggs, our local bobby, is retired, but it was great when he was around. Crime has spread to the countryside in a big way. Do you know the farmers can't even leave their combine harvesters out in the field at night? One farmer found they had pinched the whole thing, dismantled it and shipped it off. The newspapers have been full of these thefts recently. Probably ended up in Bulgaria, or somewhere. I'd better check the phone for messages. Oh, there's one for you, Roy. You're wanted back in London."

"Rats. Sorry, Agatha. I'd better get the morning train. I don't like leaving you like this."

"It's all right. Charles will be back tomorrow."

Charles woke up in the morning with a temperature, a sore throat and limbs like lead.

"I've got a bad cold," he said to Gustav. "Phone Mrs. Raisin at her office and tell her I can't see her today."

Gustav did not want to phone Agatha. He disapproved of her. He thought her a nasty, pushy sort of woman. Charles, he knew, found her attractive and he didn't want to find one day that Agatha was the new mistress of Barfield House. On the other hand, if he didn't phone, Charles would be furious with him.

So he compromised by leaving a curt message with the temp who answered the phone at the agency: "Sir Charles does not feel like seeing Mrs. Raisin."

Agatha, on receiving the message, was furious. The temp thought she had been speaking to Sir Charles personally.

Then Bill Wong called to say they were withdrawing the police protection. No, he said, they weren't much farther, but they were pursuing several leads.

After he had rung off, Agatha decided to visit Mrs. Laggat-Brown. Everything had started at the manor. Maybe if she asked some more questions, she might get an idea. Maybe Jason had talked to his future mother-in-law about his father's friends.

A brisk gale was blowing the clouds across a large sky as Agatha motored to Herris Cum Magna.

Catherine Laggat-Brown answered the door. "Oh, it's you," she said, looking flustered. "I was just about to phone you. Come in."

Once they were both seated, Catherine asked nervously, "Can I get you something? Tea? Coffee?"

"Nothing, thank you. What did you want to tell me?"

"I no longer need your services. I have decided to leave it all to the police. As Jeremy has pointed out, they have the resources which you do not have."

"But he said nothing about it when we had dinner last night!" exclaimed Agatha.

Catherine's eyes widened. "You had dinner with Jeremy last night! He told me he was meeting a business friend."

"I suppose I could be regarded as a business friend," said Agatha.

Catherine stood up. "Send me your bill. I do not want to see you again."

"But don't you want to know who shot at your daughter?"

"As I said, the police can deal with it. Now go! And keep away from my husband."

"He's not your husband. You're divorced."

"We're getting married again next month. Didn't he tell you?"

Agatha drove off, feeling furious. What was that snake Laggat-Brown on about, to have dinner with her and not mention a word of her contract being cancelled? She decided to go up to London and see him. She stopped her car and took out a train timetable. There was a train due to leave Moreton in fifteen minutes. She sped off and just managed to board the train as it was pulling out.

At Paddington, Agatha took a taxi to Fetter Lane, got out and began to search up and down for Jeremy's import/export business. She phoned Patrick and said, "Have you got the number in Fetter Lane of Laggat-Brown's business?"

He gave it to her. Agatha walked along and saw, in a dark doorway that she had already passed, "Asterix Import/Export." She climbed up a narrow, dusty staircase to the top floor, where there was a frosted glass door with "Asterix" painted on it in gold letters.

She knocked, but there was no reply.

She retreated to the landing below, where there was a sign on the door indicating it was the office of *Cutie* magazine.

She opened the door and went in. A receptionist with gelled hair and Gothic make-up stared at her indifferently.

"I want to ask about the import/export business upstairs," said Agatha. "There's no one there."

"Hardly ever is," said the girl laconically. "There was a secretary, but I ain't seen her in ages."

"What did she look like?"

"La-di-da. Yaw-yaw voice. Blonde hair. But they're all blonde these days. So naff." And she touched a finger to her own black hair complacently.

Agatha thanked her and retreated. She tried a solicitor's office on the floor below. A secretary there said she thought no one worked at Asterix anymore. "There was a lot of coming and going a year ago," she said. "Lot of visitors. But lately, there's been nothing."

Agatha then tried the sandwich shop on the ground floor, but the Greeks who ran it said they were too busy to notice anyone other than their customers.

She wanted to see Jeremy. She realized she wanted him to smile at her and tell her he had said nothing of the kind and it was all Catherine's idea. Agatha had fallen a little in love with Jeremy. She went to a doorway across the street and waited and waited to see if he would arrive. At last, she glanced at her watch and realized that if she caught the five-o'clock commuter train, he might be on it.

She went to Paddington. But once she had boarded the train, one of the very long ones run by the Great Western Railway, she could see no sign of him.

Charles drifted in and out of sleep, and by evening decided he was feeling well enough to get up for a little.

Gustav tenderly helped him into his armchair in the study and poured him a brandy.

"I've prepared a light supper of roast quail for you," said Gustav. "You should try to eat something. Are you sure you don't want me to call a doctor?"

"No, it's just a bad cold. Didn't Agatha call?"

"There's been no call from Mrs. Raisin."

Selfish, thought Charles sulkily. She might have sent me flowers.

Agatha arrived home to find Bill Wong waiting outside for her. "Don't be alarmed," said Bill. "It's a social call."

"Come in," urged Agatha. "We haven't had a chance of a proper talk in ages."

Bill followed her through to the kitchen. "You never use that dining room of yours."

"If this case ever gets solved, I'll give a dinner party. You can come and bring a girl."

"I don't have a girl at the moment. The work gets more and more, and if I set up a date I usually have to break it."

"Coffee?"

"I suppose it's safe now that Emma's inside, but she won't stand trial. She's really flipped. They tried their best to get sense out of her. At one point she even tried to claim she'd hired Mulligan to bump you off, but then she relapsed into rambling incoherently. But of course, the powers that be want to believe her and get the case closed. Which leaves us with the shooting at the manor."

"I went up to Jeremy Laggat-Brown's office today," said Agatha, plugging in the kettle. "Oh, I've got some biscuits." And seeing the look of apprehension on Bill's face, she added, "No, not mine. Doris baked them."

"PC Darren Boyd, the good-looking one who was on duty at your cottage during the day, was quite upset to be called off. He said he'd never been so pampered in all his life. You wouldn't find anything at that office?"

"Why?"

"He's closed down the business. Taken early retirement."

"Can he afford to do that?"

"Well, his ex is loaded and they're getting married again."

"I thought he was a charming man. Now I'm beginning to think he's a rat."

"Yes, but a rat who is devoted to his daughter."

"And nothing bad in his background?"

"No. We checked out all his import/export business and interviewed his clients. He's exactly what he says he is."

"Catherine Laggat-Brown's taken me off the case. Yet, I had

dinner with Jeremy the night before and he said nothing about it."

"Oho, have you been dating him?"

"No, Roy was there. He was interested in what we'd found out but I couldn't tell him anything about Mulligan because I was told not to. Nothing in Harrison Peterson's background?"

"We're still digging, finding out who he made friends with in prison, that sort of thing."

"Let me know when you find anything." Agatha set two cups of coffee and a plate of biscuits on the table.

"I'm not supposed to." Hodge climbed up Bill's trouser leg and settled on his lap.

"Funny how much these cats love you. How are your parents?"

"Mother's got bad arthritis in her hip. She had this pain for ages but she wouldn't get the hip x-rayed and now she's got to queue up for a hip operation."

Agatha's hip gave a sharp twinge and she thought, I can't have arthritis. Surely only old people get it.

Bill finished his coffee, ate two biscuits and left, saying "Look after yourself. In fact, Agatha, stick to divorces and missing dogs and cats. You're off the Laggat-Brown case. So leave it that way."

Agatha made herself a supper of lasagne in the microwave. She overdid it and it was stuck to the sides of the plastic tray, but she scraped off what she could. She decided to cook up some fish for the cats, and after the fish was cooked switched off the gas and went upstairs.

She had a long hot bath, opened her bedroom window, and went to bed.

184

Agatha awoke with a start. There was a scratching and yowling from the thatch above her head. She leaped out of bed and opened the bedroom window wide and leaned out. Her cats were up on the roof. She could not see them but she recognized their cries.

Agatha pulled her head in and was just about to switch on her bedside light when she smelt gas. North Sea gas does not have the same strong smell as the old coal gas, but she knew it was gas all the same. She hurried down to the kitchen, trying to breathe as little as possible.

The gas under the fish pot was switched full on. She switched it off and opened the kitchen door and breathed in great lungfuls of fresh air.

It was then she realized that when she opened the kitchen door the burglar alarm had not gone off.

But her overriding thought was to rescue her cats.

She got an extension ladder out of the shed at the bottom of the garden, and carrying it up the path, placed it against the thatch and climbed up.

Agatha called to her cats, who approached her cautiously. She managed to get hold of Hodge, and Boswell leaped onto her shoulder. Agatha eased down the ladder with the cats and collapsed on the grass, holding her head in her hands and feeling sick.

Then she went indoors and opened the front door and all the windows before she phoned the police.

PC Boyd, accompanied by PC Betty Howse, arrived. At first they were sure that Agatha had simply forgotten to light the gas.

"It doesn't light automatically," said Agatha. "You have to push that button there to ignite it. And why didn't the burglar alarm go off?"

Boyd put on a pair of thin gloves and lifted the cover off the main burglar alarm box.

"It's switched off," he said over his shoulder. "Are you sure you didn't do it?"

"Absolutely not!"

"But when you came in this evening, it must have sounded before you punched in the code."

"Come to think of it, it didn't. Bill Wong was with me and I was talking to him and didn't notice."

"That would be Detective Sergeant Bill Wong?"

"Yes, we're friends."

"Who else has keys to your house?"

"Just Doris Simpson."

"I'll need her phone number."

Agatha gave it to him and he picked up the phone and called Doris. Agatha's heart sank as she heard Boyd's end of the conversation. "What repair-man? What did he look like? Did he show you any identification? Did you leave your keys lying around? Did you leave him alone at any time?"

Meanwhile Betty Howse reached up and took down the instruction manual from the control box. "What's this?" she demanded sharply, pointing to the numbers "5936" written on top of the instruction manual.

"It's the code," mumbled Agatha. "I kept forgetting it, so I wrote it down."

Meanwhile, Boyd ended his interrogation of Doris. "A man saying he was from the security company who installed the burglar alarm called round when Mrs. Simpson was here. He flashed some sort of card at her and she let him in. Then she said she had to get down to the shops to get some more cleaning stuff and she left the keys on the table. Time enough for him to get an impression of them. He makes sure the alarm is switched off. He then comes back when you're asleep, lets himself in. But what puzzles me is that he couldn't guarantee you wouldn't notice the alarm had been switched off. He wouldn't know that a short burst of alarm as he let himself in wouldn't wake you. He didn't have the code to switch it off quickly."

"Oh, yes, he did," said Betty and held out the instruction book with the code written on it.

"Amateurs. You, I mean," said Boyd bitterly. "So it was planned to look like an accident. The house fills with gas. You switch on a light, and, boom, you're history. Now I must ask you to leave the kitchen alone until a forensic team arrives. In fact, it would be better if you could stay with someone."

Agatha thought desperately. "I could phone Mrs. Bloxby, the vicar's wife, but it's the middle of the night and her husband would be furious. I would check into an hotel, but they probably wouldn't let me bring my cats and I don't want to leave them here. I know, I'll get Doris to drop in and look after the cats and then I'll book into some hotel."

"We need to know which one."

"There's a big one outside Bourton-on-the-Water called The Cotswold."

"Phone them now."

So Agatha phoned and was assured of a room. She went upstairs and got dressed and packed a bag. Then she put her cats into the large cat box and drove round to Doris Simpson. Doris was still awake and full of apologies. "Honestly, he was such a meek-looking little man. I didn't think for a moment there was anything wrong. Of course I'll look after the cats."

Agatha drove off in the direction of Bourton-on-the Water, feeling numb. Why was she considered such a danger? She didn't know much, and what she knew was surely considerably less than what the police knew. In the hotel room, she unpacked her few belongings, undressed and climbed into bed. She lay shivering despite the central heating. She felt they, whoever they were, were not going to give up. The only solution, surely, was to leave the country for an extended holiday and let everyone know she had left so that the murderer or murderers would no longer think her a threat.

She fell into an uneasy sleep and woke up in the morning remembering her dreams and feeling she had spent the night in some sort of Shakespearian play, with first murderer and second murderer waiting in the wings.

Agatha craved the soothing presence of Mrs. Bloxby, but first she drove to her cottage. A forensic team was working outside like so many figures from science fiction in their white hooded suits, gloves and white bags tied over their boots.

One of Agatha's favourite programmes on television was *CSI*—Crime Investigators. Now she wondered if that was really how American forensic teams went on, treading all over crime sites in their normal clothes and shaking their own hair and DNA all over the place.

She left her car and walked up to the vicarage.

Mrs. Bloxby let her in and said that as the day was fine, they could sit in the garden where Agatha could have a cigarette, mindful of her husband's complaint, "Keep that bloody woman and her cigarettes out of the house."

"I hear a forensic team are back at your cottage. What happened?"

So Agatha told her, and when she had finished, Mrs. Bloxby

said, "I would have thought Bill Wong might have noticed the burglar alarm wasn't on."

"No reason to," sighed Agatha. "I never think about other people's alarm systems, so why should he?"

"What are you going to do now?"

"I don't know. I can't think. But I've a feeling that whoever is behind this won't stop now. I keep going over and over it. Maybe I do know something that's frightened whoever. If only I could think what. My neck's rigid with tension and I feel like shit. Sorry. I know you don't like bad language."

"Because I'm a vicar's wife? Nonsense. I hear much worse every day. Besides, have you noticed it's a must in every American action film—two men, one black, one white, leap in front of an exploding building, shouting, 'Oh, sh-i-t!' I think you should go for a massage. There's marvellous man in Stow called Richard Rasdall. He could give you a relaxing massage. I'll phone him if you like."

"Might be a good idea. I'm not doing anything else and I've a pain in the neck, which is exactly what the police think I am. Oh, Lord, they're probably phoning the hotel asking me to go to police headquarters and make a statement."

"Go to Richard first and then you'll feel more up to it."

Mrs. Bloxby went into the vicarage to phone. Agatha suddenly wished she could stay in this pleasant garden among the late roses forever. The world outside was an ugly, threatening place.

The vicar's wife returned and said, "He can take you in half an hour. If you leave now, you'll make it easily provided you can find a parking place."

"Where do I go?"

"If you get a place in the parking spot at the market cross,

189

you walk up past Lloyd's bank as if you're going to the church. There's sweetie shop called The Honey Pot. It's in there."

"In a sweetie shop!"

"He works upstairs. You'll meet his wife, Lyn. Such a nice pretty woman. Lovely family."

As Agatha drove to Stow-on-the Wold, she noticed the sun had gone in and the day was becoming as dark as her mood. At the back car-park by the market cross, cars were circling around like so many prowling metal animals searching for places. Agatha saw that a woman was about to reverse into a place and quickly drove straight into it.

She sat there with the windows up and switched on the radio for a few moments to drown out the yells of frustration from the woman driver. Then she got out, feeling suddenly stiff and old and beaten.

Agatha trudged up to The Honey Pot and went inside.

ELEVEN

†

AGATHA stood just inside the door and looked around. The little shop was bathed in a golden light. There were glass shelves of delicious-looking chocolates, other shelves with little bags of Cotswold fudge, boxes of biscuits, and toys. But there were also little "fairy" dresses for small girls: magical creations which looked as if they had been made out of gossamer. And the shoes! Tiny sparkling sequinned shoes, shoes such as Dorothy wore in *The Wizard of Oz*.

What would it be like, wondered Agatha, to be a little girl whose parents were so loving, so indulgent, so proud of their child's looks that they would buy her one of those beautiful dresses?

"Are you Mrs. Raisin?"

Agatha focused on the woman standing behind the small counter. "I'm Lyn Rasdall," she said. "You've come to see Richard, haven't you?"

"Yes," said Agatha. "This place looks like something out of Harry Potter."

"Mrs. Raisin!"

A tall, handsome man with deep-set eyes had appeared at the back of the shop.

"I'm Richard."

"Hullo," said Agatha. "Where do I go?"

"Up the stairs," said Richard, "and get on board. First door on the left. Take all your clothes off except your knickers and cover yourself with the towel."

Agatha went upstairs and found herself in a large bathroom with a massage table in the centre. Soft music was playing and scented candles were burning on a sideboard.

She took off her clothes down to her pair of plain white knickers. She climbed up onto the table and covered herself with a large bath sheet.

"On board?" called Richard from outside the door.

"Yes," said Agatha.

The massage started with her feet. Agatha lay there and fretted while Richard told her about his work in Bosnia, treating unfortunate women who had been tortured and raped as part of his work for the Healing Hands Society.

"I've been so stressed out about a case I've been working on," said Agatha. "I'm a private detective. Somehow it all started when I was in Paris during that heat wave."

"So I hear. I had a Frenchwoman here after the summer. Recovering alcoholic. Said she could hardly get to her reunions or whatever they call AA meetings over there."

Gradually Agatha began to relax. When she turned over and he began to work on her back, she could feel all her troubles melting away. Her brain felt calm and rested. Bits of the case floated in and out of her head. Paris. The visit and meeting Phyllis Hepper chattering on about some handsome drunkard who'd got sober. Reunion! Jeremy Laggat-Brown had said to the hotel reception that he was going to a reunion, not to see friends or anything like that, but to a reunion. Felicity Felliet. Jeremy had a la-di-da blonde secretary. Her mind suddenly seemed to take a great leap. Supposing, just supposing, that Jeremy had found some drunk or recovering alcoholic who looked enough like him to take his place. Perhaps even a hardened alcoholic would stay dry for the short time necessary for the impersonation if the money was enough. If not a drunk, then someone else who looked like him. And wait a bit. There was something else. Charles had spoken to Jeremy in French. Jeremy had said he didn't understand him because Charles's French was atrocious. But, thought Agatha, with another mental jolt, Charles's French was surely excellent. The French police didn't have the slightest trouble in understanding him.

"What's up?" asked Richard. "You've gone all tense."

Agatha turned over and sat up. "I've got to get out of here!"

"I haven't finished."

"No, got to go. Must go."

Richard dived out of the room as a half-naked Agatha tumbled off the table and began scrabbling into her clothes.

When she ran down the stairs, he was standing with his wife in the shop. "How much?" asked Agatha.

"Fifteen pounds."

The business woman in Agatha came to the fore. "Is that because you didn't finish?"

"No, that's my fee."

"My dear man, it's too little." Agatha fished the exact money out of her wallet and fled out of the shop.

"What was up with her?" asked Lyn.

"Blessed if I know," said Richard. "I think she's a sandwich short of a picnic."

Agatha drove to the hotel and checked out. The police had left several messages asking her to report to headquarters.

She then set off for Barfield House.

Gustav answered the door. "He's ill," he said, "and doesn't want visitors."

"Charles!" shouted Agatha at the top of her voice as the door began to close in her face.

"Who is it, Gustav?" came Charles's voice.

Gustav cast a look of loathing at Agatha and said reluctantly, "Mrs. Raisin."

"Show her in."

"Push off, Gustav," snarled Agatha, edging past him.

"I'm in the study," called Charles.

Agatha walked in. "I told Gustav to phone you and tell you I was ill," grumbled Charles.

"Oh, it was Gustav, was it? The message I got from the temp was that you had called with the message you didn't want to see me, nothing else."

"She probably got it wrong. Most of these temps are hopeless."

"I don't think so. Anyway, listen!"

Agatha told him first about the latest attempt on her life. Then she said, "This is very important. You addressed Jeremy in French in the restaurant. What did you say?"

"I said he had better stop romancing you if he wanted to be reconciled with his ex-wife. He pretended not to understand me."

"I don't think he was pretending. Listen to this."

Agatha outlined all her new ideas. "You're forgetting one thing," said Charles. "It was his own daughter who got the death threat. It was his own daughter who was shot at."

"Wait a bit. Bill Wong told me he'd packed up his business. He says he hopes to remarry Catherine. She's loaded. Now just suppose he wants her money without her. Perhaps the death threat to the daughter was a blind and he really meant to shoot his wife."

"Aggie, it's impossible to prove any of this."

"Well, I'm going to Paris and I'm going to see Phyllis and get an introduction to the handsome drunk. If I can get him to say he impersonated Jeremy, then I've got him. In fact, I'm driving to Heathrow now."

"I'm coming with you. What about Birmingham? It's closer, easier to park, and they've got flights to Paris. Gustav? Pack a bag."

Charles moaned the whole flight and clutched his head, complaining that his ears were bursting and saying they should have taken the train. "I should have known not to fly with a cold."

Agatha largely ignored him because she was turning ideas over and over in her head. If they drew a blank, if Jeremy had not got someone to impersonate him, it would be a wasted trip. She edged Phyllis's card out of her wallet. She should have phoned in advance.

Charles began to recover on the taxi ride to the hotel. They were going to stay at the same one as before. The sun was shining down on Paris, and as they neared the centre of the city, people were sitting out on the terraces in the sunlight.

At the hotel, Agatha was pleased to find that this time they could have a room each. She phoned Phyllis and was relieved to find her at home and asked if she would like to join them for lunch.

Phyllis said she was busy but could meet them for a coffee in the afternoon. Agatha suggested the Village Ronsard in Maubert where they had met before, and Phyllis said she would meet them at three o'clock.

"It's only eleven," said Agatha when she had hung up. "Let's go and see if we can find Felicity."

"You go," groaned Charles. "I'm off to my room to lie down. Honestly, Aggie, I'm shattered."

The old Agatha would have blasted him, called him a wimp, but the new Agatha was suddenly aware of the value of friends, so she said gruffly, "That's all right. I'll let you know how I get on."

She unpacked her few belongings and then went out and took a cab to the Rue Saint-Honoré. Once more she entered the salon.

The woman she had met before approached her, her dark eyes flicking up and down Agatha's rather crumpled trouser suit. Agatha had two Armani trouser suits, but the one she was wearing was a cheap one she had bought in Evesham. She could almost feel the woman pricing it in her mind and then dismissing it and its owner.

"I am here to see Felicity Felliet," said Agatha, suddenly wishing she had insisted that Charles come with her. Charles had a reasonable explanation for calling on Felicity, being a friend of her father, but Agatha had not.

But the woman said, "Mees Felicity is not with us. She left."

"When?"

A little Gallic shrug and a spreading of the fingers. "Last week."

"Have you an address for her in Paris?"

"Wait. I look."

Agatha waited and fretted. Her brilliant idea was beginning to seem more and more far-fetched.

The woman returned and handed Agatha a slip of paper. It gave an address in the Rue Madame.

Agatha again hailed a taxi and found herself once more being borne across the river, but this time to the Sixth Arrondissement, near the impressive baroque church of Saint Sulpice.

She paid off the taxi and looked up at the tall building. It was one of those infuriating entry systems where you needed a code to get into the building.

There was a window at the side of the door. Hoping it was the concierge, Agatha rapped on it. The curtain twitched and a face looked out. After a few moments the door swung open. A small birdlike woman stood there with a pencil thrust through her frizzy hair.

"Miss Felliet?" asked Agatha.

"Numéro dix-sept."

Agatha looked at her in bewilderment. "I don't understand French."

The concierge retreated into her room off the hall and reappeared with a piece of paper of which she had written "17." Then she pointed upwards.

Agatha went over to the lift, one of those old-fashioned French ones like a gilt cage. The concierge followed her and pressed the top button. The gate slowly closed and the lift creaked upwards. When it stopped on the top floor, she got out and looked around. The building was very quiet. No cries of children or smells of cooking. Must be expensive, thought Agatha. Only the rich apartment dweller could afford this sort of hush.

There was one door with a bell-push beside it. Agatha rang the bell. She heard sounds of movement inside. Then the door was opened and a tall bespectacled man stood there.

"Can I help you?" he asked. The accent was American.

"I'm looking for Felicity Felliet."

"No one here of that name, but I've only just moved in. Come in."

Agatha walked in and looked around. There were packing cases everywhere. French windows opened out onto a balcony and a view of the rooftops of Paris.

He went over to a desk. "I've got the name of the estate agent here. Maybe if you tried them you could find out where she has gone. I never saw her but I assume she must have been the previous tenant. I was lucky to get a place with an elevator. The higher you go, the cheaper it gets and even cheaper if there isn't an elevator, but I didn't fancy carrying everything up miles of stairs."

"How far from here is this estate agent?"

"Turn left as you go out and walk straight down to Saint Germain and then turn right. It's about one block along."

Agatha thanked him and creaked down in the maddeningly slow lift. She spent some time figuring out how to open the street door. She knocked at the concierge's door but there was no reply. Then she saw a button under the light switch and pressed it. The door gave a click and Agatha pulled it open. As it was one of those enormous carved wooden doors they have in buildings in Paris, she had to use both hands.

She turned left and walked, stopping occasionally to ask people for directions by simply saying, "Saint Germain?" and following where they pointed.

At the estate agent's, there was a wait while the people in the front office went through to the back to find someone who spoke English.

A neat little Frenchman appeared and listened courteously, his head cocked to one side like a sparrow, while she asked if he knew the whereabouts of Felicity Felliet.

"Her lease was up last week," he said, "and she said she did not want to renew it. She said she was returning to England."

So that's a dead end, thought Agatha. She's probably back with her parents.

By the time Agatha and Charles met Phyllis, Agatha was beginning to feel her whole idea was ridiculous. But Phyllis listened eagerly, exclaiming that it all sounded very exciting. "What is this Jeremy Laggat-Brown like?" she asked.

"He is well-built with a tanned face, very bright blue eyes and thick curly white hair."

"There's someone like that who goes to meetings. Jean-Paul. He came off the streets and looked a mess, but after he sobered up, he didn't look at all like the same person."

"Could we meet him?"

"Actually I have his phone number." Phyllis took out her mobile and dialled and then proceeded to speak in French. When she rang off, she said triumphantly, "He lives near here and is coming to join us. He won't be long."

Agatha began to feel excited. Oh, please let this Jean-Paul be the spitting image of Jeremy.

Ten minutes later, Phyllis exclaimed, "Here he is."

Agatha swung round in her chair and her heart sank. Jean-Paul had white hair streaked with grey and his eyes were blue-grey. He was tall but had a stoop. But his main feature was a very large, very prominent nose.

He joined them and listened carefully while Charles and Phyllis, speaking in French, explained what they were looking for. Agatha sat in frustrated silence, privately vowing to take French lessons as soon as this wretched case was over. If ever.

Charles said, "It's certainly not him and he can't think of anyone it might be."

Agatha's heart sank. The police would be looking for her because she hadn't turned up to give a statement. If they checked the airports, they would find she had left the country and would alert the French police.

Phyllis, Jean-Paul and Charles proceeded to chat in French while Agatha sat in a sullen, worried silence.

When they at last said goodbye, Charles suggested that as their plane wasn't until the morning, they might as well take a walk along the Seine and visit Notre Dame.

"Seen it," said Agatha crossly.

"Well, see it again."

They turned off Place Maubert and down Rue Frédéric Sauton. "Oh, look," said Charles. "There's an AA office, right across the road from that Lebanese restaurant. Shall I ask there? I mean, Phyllis only goes to English-speaking meetings."

"If we must," sighed Agatha. "But I'm beginning to feel very silly. I mean, why would he get a drunk to impersonate him when he could possibly have found someone sober?"

"Maybe it was hard to find someone sober who looked like him."

Charles pressed the bell and spoke into the intercom and they were buzzed in. Agatha sank down onto a chair and stared numbly into space while Charles rattled away in French.

And then she noticed that Charles was beginning to look excited. She straightened up. "What's going on? What's he saying?"

"Listen to this one, Aggie. There's a clochard—you know, a drunk—who passes his time with the other drunks by the fountain on Place Maubert. Sometimes he's sober, sometimes not. He's usually there in the evenings. His nickname is Milord. He has white hair and blue eyes. He occasionally comes down to this office, swearing he wants to get sober, but he never manages it."

"Do you think he could have managed it for long enough to keep up a pretence?"

Charles spoke in French again. When he heard the reply, he turned to Agatha. "They say he might if there was enough money in it for him."

When they left, they were both too excited to do anything other than go to the Métro brasserie, which had outside tables facing the fountain, and wait.

They waited and waited. They could hear the great bells of Notre Dame beginning to chime at five-thirty. The brasserie began to fill up and people dropped in for coffee on their road home from work. There were still plenty of tourists around. Cycling tours glided past and then roller-blading tours. Around them, American, Dutch and German voices mingled with the French ones.

As dusk fell, several drunks could be seen sitting at the

fountain, some with their worldly goods in shopping carts, others with their dogs.

And then they saw a white-haired man approaching. He sat down on the edge of the fountain and pulled a bottle from the ragged pocket of his jacket and took a swig.

Charles paid the bill and they got up and approached him.

Charles began to speak while Agatha's heart beat faster. Milord had the same blue eyes and white hair, though his once-handsome face was marred with red veins. Charles turned to Agatha. "He says he'll sober up for money," he said. "He's called Luke."

"Do anything for money," said Luke in perfect English.

"We'd like to ask you a few questions," said Agatha. "Let's go somewhere quiet. Are you very drunk?"

"Not yet," said Luke amiably. "Just woke up."

"We'll head down to the Seine," said Charles, "and sit down by the river."

They went down to the river and walked down the steps and sat on a bench facing the floodlit bulk of Notre Dame.

"How much?" asked Luke.

Agatha thought quickly. "One hundred euros."

He shrugged. "I got a thousand from the other one."

Agatha had collected exactly a thousand euros from a post office on her road to Birmingham Airport. She had spent some of it but knew she could get more with one of her bank cards at a cash-dispensing machine.

"All right," she said. "But you've got to make a statement to the police."

"No, that's out."

"Look, tell us the story. I don't think you've anything to fear from the police. I mean, he didn't say, 'Impersonate me while I go and murder my wife,' did he?"

"No, he said it was a joke, that was all."

"Then you have nothing to fear. One thousand euros."

There was a long silence. A bateau mouche sailed past, lighting up their faces and turning the plane trees on the quay above them bright green.

He reached for his bottle, but Charles said firmly, "No drink."

He shrugged and then began to talk. His name was Luke Field, son of a French mother and an English father. His father had left them and his mother had moved back to Paris from England. He had worked as a graphic artist but had been fired from a succession of jobs. This Englishman had approached him and had suggested he help him play a trick. Luke had agreed because he thought with the money, he could get sober and get a job again. The man called Jeremy had taken him to a flat in the Rue Madame.

"Top flat?" asked Agatha breathlessly.

"Yes. There was a blonde woman there. He called her Felicity." She had left soon after Luke arrived. Jeremy had gone back to the hotel and reappeared with one of his suits, shoes and shirt and tie. Luke actually had a passport, although he said he often thought of selling it for money. He was bathed and shaved and his face was made up to cover the broken veins. He had to practise imitating Jeremy's voice and manner. The deal was that he was to stay at the hotel one night. Then this Jeremy would take his passport and fly to England while Luke was to follow the next day on Jeremy's passport. Once there, he was to phone Jeremy, who would meet him. They would exchange passports and then Luke would get paid and fly back.

"But why did you speak French at the hotel?" asked Charles. "Laggat-Brown didn't know any French."

"I didn't know that," said Luke. "He told me his French was excellent, but he spoke to me the whole time in English. I thought I'd go to a meeting and then go straight to bed to keep me sober."

But then Luke became truculent. He said he didn't want to have anything to do with the police.

"All right," said Agatha, "but come with us to our hotel and I'll get you the money. It's in the hotel safe."

And please let the French police be waiting for us, Agatha prayed silently.

But her heart sank when they arrived at the hotel. Not a uniform in sight. "Come up to my room," she said to Luke. She felt if she stalled for time, they might arrive. Why was Charles coming with them? Couldn't he go to his own room and phone the police from there? But she was frightened to do anything to scare Luke off.

Once in her room, she went to the safe and pulled out her wallet. After her last experience, she had decided to carry as little money with her as possible when she went out.

She slowly began to count out the money and then stopped half-way. "I don't really feel I should pay you anything because you won't go to the police. In fact," she said, scooping up the money and putting it back in her wallet, "your information is no use to us without a statement."

Luke looked at her hungrily. He was dying for a drink. Did he really want to go back to work? Winter was drawing closer and he thought another winter on the streets might kill him.

But the thought of the police terrified him. They would probably accuse him of being in league with this killer.

There came a peremptory knock at the door and a voice called in English, "Police. Open up!"

Luke hung his head. The fates had made up his mind for him.

TWELVE

✝

AGATHA was never to forget that long night of questioning
and more questioning. Then she was told that when they got off
the plane in the morning, a police car would be waiting at Birmingham for them.

She and Charles were both groggy with lack of sleep when
they arrived at Birmingham Airport. And got into the waiting police car.

"They've got to let us rest," grumbled Agatha. "I can't take
much more of this."

They both fell asleep as the police car raced towards Mircester. At police headquarters, they were told they would be interrogated separately.

Agatha was to be interviewed by Fother from the Special
Branch and Detective Inspector Wilkes.

"Before we begin," said Agatha urgently, as a policeman was putting a tape in the recoding machine, "have you arrested Laggat-Brown?"

"Yes, he's been brought in for questioning."

"I suppose he's saying he got Luke to impersonate him for a joke."

"He tried, but we took that office of his apart. He was still renting it, although he no longer uses it. Under the floorboards, we found the sniper rifle and a supply of timers. Now, Mrs. Raisin, let us begin. We find it most odd that you suddenly thought he might have found someone to impersonate him. We think you have been holding back evidence from the police."

"It was just an idea," said Agatha wearily. She told the story of Phyllis and the recovered alcoholic.

"But why Felicity Felliet?"

"The Felliets were deeply humiliated by the loss of their ancestral home. I wondered, simply because of the Paris connection, if she had been in on the plot in any way. Have you got her?"

"We're looking. She seems to have disappeared and her parents have not had any contact with her. But we find it hard to believe that you just plucked this idea out of thin air. Are you sure you weren't in league with Laggat-Brown and that the relationship went sour?"

"No," shouted Agatha. "And get me a cup of coffee before I fall asleep."

The questioning went on for hours, and just when Agatha thought she really could not bear any more of it, they told her she could go home, but not to leave the country.

Agatha met Charles as he was leaving as well. "Do we need a police car?" asked Agatha.

"No, I gave them my car keys and told them to collect my car from the airport."

"My car's out at your place."

"I'll come over tonight with Gustav. He can drive yours and then I'll take him back with me."

Agatha let herself into her cottage. She checked the cats' food bowls to make sure Doris had given them something, went straight up and fell face-down on the bed and into a deep sleep, only to be awakened four hours later with the sound of the doorbell ringing.

She debated whether to let it ring, but then decided it might be Mrs. Bloxby. She trudged wearily down the stairs and opened the door. Bill Wong stood there, holding a bunch of flowers.

"You look as if you've been through the wars," said Bill.

"Flowers. How lovely. Come in, Bill. What on earth's been happening?"

He followed her through to the kitchen. "It's like this. I had a time of it explaining about how your mad ideas and intuitions had worked out in the past. Laggat-Brown cracked when they produced the rifle and timers.

"It seemed he made his money supplying timers for bombs to the Provisional IRA and other terrorist groups. Then he met Felicity Felliet and fell in love. He wanted out of the terrorist business and she wanted her home back. He really did mean to shoot his wife.

"Then Felicity heard that Charles had been round to see her parents, asking questions about her. She checked up old newspaper files on you, Agatha, and persuaded Laggat-Brown you were more dangerous than the police. He didn't want to do the hit himself, but he had plenty of contacts and employed Mulligan to do it.

"He then decided to remarry his wife and after a convenient time arrange a death for her that would look like an accident. After the attempt to gas you failed, he became wary of getting anyone to try to kill you—for the moment, that was.

"Employing Luke, the drunk, was a spot of luck for him, or so he thought. It was Felicity who saw Luke one day and noticed the remarkable resemblance."

"She's beginning to sound like Lady Macbeth."

"Yes," said Bill, "she seems to have been a major player in the whole business. She worked for a while as Laggat-Brown's secretary and then they both decided it would be better if she moved to Paris so that there would be less chance of anyone seeing them together.

"After he had finally got rid of his wife, he would inherit her money, marry Felicity and Felicity would get her old home back."

"And what about Harrison Peterson?"

"It turns out Harrison Peterson was a bagman for the Provisional IRA, moving funds around the world, taking cash to the Colombian terrorists, that sort of thing. He wanted out of the game, too, and was going to talk to the police, after he had talked to Patrick. It was Laggat-Brown who had your phone bugged. He heard Patrick's message and knew Harrison had to be eliminated. He also knew he would have to do it himself because Harrison would trust him enough to let him in."

"And no one has any idea of where Felicity is at the moment?"

"No, but I don't think she'd dare try anything. I don't think she cared a rap for Laggat-Brown. I think she was simply using him to get her home back. Her poor parents are devastated. Don't worry. We're looking for her and Interpol are looking for her and Special Branch are trying to track her down. The only sad thing is that you'll get no credit for solving this case."

"Why not?"

"Well, to quote Fother, 'I'm damned if the papers are going to know that some dotty female from a provincial detective agency cracked a case that the Special Branch could not.' "

"I could phone them myself," said Agatha.

"Not before the trial, you can't."

"I suppose not. I'll phone Patrick and tell him I'm taking the day off tomorrow. All I want to do is sleep and then get my face and hair done."

"You'll be glad to know that an officer is going to be on duty outside your door tonight and the handsome Darren Boyd takes over from him tomorrow."

After he had left, Agatha luxuriated in a long hot bath. Then, putting on a dressing-gown, she went back downstairs and put a packet of spaghetti bolognaise into the microwave for her dinner. When she had finished eating, she rose and let the cats out into the garden for a little. Then she let them in again and locked up and went back to bed.

But sleep was a long time coming. Somewhere out there in the world was Felicity Felliet and Agatha was sure she would be hell-bent on revenge.

Charles called early next morning with Gustav to return her car and said he would be back that evening and that there must be something restorative in police coffee, for his cold had completely disappeared.

Agatha spent the day getting a complete facial and followed it up by getting her hair tinted brown.

Then she returned to find Charles parked outside, waiting for her. Charles was always amazed that Agatha's foul diet of microwaved meals left her with thick glossy hair and perfect skin.

"Forgot my key. I see handsome Boyd's outside, sitting at a little table of goodies."

"The village women spoil him. What now?"

"Maybe we'd better go and see George; least we can do."

George Felliet was furious with them. Charles had to listen to a passionate tirade about snakes in the grass and false friends. Waiting until George had exhausted himself, Charles said mildly, "You have to face up to the fact that she's guilty."

George suddenly collapsed into a chair. "She hated leaving the manor," he said. "Even as a little girl, she couldn't understand that the money was running out. Kept demanding expensive things—clothes, the latest in computers, that sort of thing. But I never thought she would go this far."

"And you haven't heard from her?"

"Not a word."

Crystal Felliet came into the house and glared at them. "Get out!" she shouted.

"But Crystal . . ." Charles began.

"OUT!" she screamed.

Agatha and Charles left hurriedly. In the car, Agatha said, "Do you think they'd hide their daughter if she went to them?"

"Hard to say. I think that's an unmarked police car across the road."

"Are you staying the night?"

"I'd like to, but I've got farm business to attend to. You'll be all right with the police guard on the door."

In the psychiatric prison the next morning, Emma Comfrey continued to wander about talking to herself. Emma's brain had cleared up a few days before, but she continued to act mad because she did not want to be judged fit to stand trial.

In the past few days she had managed to keep up the pretence of insanity during interviews with various psychiatrists. But that afternoon, she was presented with a new psychiatrist, a woman with small eyes and glossy brown hair. She reminded Emma forcibly of Agatha Raisin—Agatha Raisin, whom Emma blamed for all her troubles.

Emma dribbled and smiled vacantly while all the time her mind was racing. Convinced she could not break through the wall of Emma's insanity, the psychiatrist left, and was replaced with a nurse.

"Now, dearie," said the nurse. "Take your medicine."

She held out a little dish with a few pills on it.

Emma stared at her vacantly. "Here. I'll help you. Here's the glass of water. Here's the first pill."

Emma's eyes drifted past her to her tray containing a syringe of tranquillizer, used for subduing patients who turned violent. Emma had seen such a one used on a patient just the other day. She took the glass of water and threw it in the nurse's face, grabbed the tranquillizer syringe while clamping her hand over the nurse's mouth, and plunged the needle in. She held on grimly until at last she felt the nurse go limp in her arms.

She removed the nurse's white coat and outer clothes and

shoes, stripped off her hospital garments and put them all on, pinning the nurse's identification card on her white coat.

Then she dragged the nurse over to the bed and rolled her onto it and covered her right up with the blankets.

Emma was not considered any risk, so there was no guard outside the door. She picked up the nurse's clipboard and made her way out, keeping her head down as if studying it as she made her way hurriedly along the corridor. She saw a doctor approaching who knew her and dived into a room which turned out to be a pharmacy.

There was a male nurse on duty. "I need a couple more tranquillizer syringes," said Emma briskly. He reluctantly put down the newspaper he had been reading, unlocked a cabinet and gave her two syringes and then produced a book. "Sign here." He had not recognized her, but nurses in a psychiatric prison came and went.

Emma glanced down at the laminated card on her bosom and signed "Jane Hopkirk," the nurse's name.

She put the syringes in her pocket and felt a key at the bottom of the pocket. The corridor outside was empty, so she took out the key and looked at it. A locker key.

Where would the lockers be? Then she nearly laughed out loud. On the wall at the end of the corridor was a plan of the hospital.

She could smell lunch being served. Hopefully that would mean that most of the nurses would be in the canteen, leaving the orderlies to take round the patients' meals.

In the locker room, she located the right one from the number on the key. Inside was a coat and a handbag. Inside the handbag were car keys.

Emma put on the coat and took the handbag. She then walked down the stairs and briskly out through the front door.

She went round to the car-park and flicked the remote control round all the cars until she saw one flash its security lights.

It was the latest Volvo. Miss Hopkirk must have money, thought Emma. She could never afford this on a nurse's salary.

There was a security pass on the windscreen, so she drove past the security guard with a wave and a smile. Once she was well out on the road, she parked at the side and rummaged through the handbag. The wallet contained over one hundred pounds. In a side pocket of the bag, to her delight, she found a pin number. She drove on to the nearest cash machine, put in a card and drew out two hundred.

They would come for her when she had done what she had to do, but Agatha Raisin would no longer be alive.

She left the car outside Mircester and bought a bicycle and then began to cycle towards Carsely through the back roads heavy with autumn foliage.

PC Boyd stretched out his long legs. The day had turned sunny again. He felt very sleepy, full of tea, home-made scones and cake.

A slim young woman wearing a business suit and with a silk scarf over her head, approached him.

"I wonder if you would like to try some of my home-made wine," she said. "Agatha's sent me from the office to pick up some papers for her. I have the keys."

"That's very kind of you."

"Do have a glass. I'm very proud of it."

"Maybe just one. Don't tell anyone. I'm not supposed to drink on duty."

"I've brought a glass." The bottle had a screw top. She unscrewed it and poured him a glass.

Boyd watched as she unlocked the door and switched off the burglar alarm. Then, when the door had closed, he smelt the glass of wine. It smelt terribly sweet. He didn't want to offend her, so he poured the contents off into a bed of winter pansies and settled back in his chair. The sun was warm, he was full of home-made goodies and in no time at all, he fell asleep.

He did not hear the door behind him open a little and then close.

Felicity Felliet went back into the kitchen and sat down to wait. She had put a heavy drug into that wine. She was glad Jeremy had left the keys to Agatha's cottage with her. The man he had hired to gas Agatha had got two sets cut, sending one to Jeremy for safekeeping in case the first attempt failed. And the silly bitch had forgotten to change her alarm code.

The cats were staring at her. Felicity opened the garden door and they ran out. She had tailed Agatha and had noticed her going into the village store. Wouldn't be long now. "I'm doing this for you, Jeremy, you loser, and to get rid of that bitch who made me lose my home," she muttered.

Agatha left the village stores carrying two cans of cat food. Her pampered cats preferred real food, but they would need to make do this one time with the commercial stuff. Agatha was tired after answering more and more questions. She suddenly decided to go and visit Mrs. Bloxby and tell her everything that had happened.

The vicar's wife listened in amazement to Agatha's story.

"I always thought that intuition of yours was a gift from God, Mrs. Raisin."

Agatha looked uncomfortable, as she always did when God was mentioned.

"Felicity Felliet is still out there."

"I think you'll be safe as long as the police keep a guard on you. Where can she run to?"

"Anywhere," said Agatha gloomily. "I bet you that one has six passports."

Emma had stopped to buy a hunting knife. Her brain felt amazingly clear and logical. But as she left the bicycle at the top of the road down into Carsely and began to walk, she could feel nagging little voices at the back of her brain. One of them belonged to her late husband. "You are a frump, Emma," he was saying. "Haven't you anything else to wear?"

She ignored the voices and walked doggedly on. She planned to stab Agatha with one of the tranquillizer syringes and then slowly cut her up. When she turned into Lilac Lane, she stopped short at the sight of the policeman, but he appeared to be asleep. She walked forwards and edged past him.

Emma was about to ring the bell, but she decided to try the door first. To her delight it opened. Agatha was at home.

She walked through to the kitchen.

A strange blonde young woman was sitting at the kitchen table.

Felicity looked at Emma and Emma looked at Felicity. Felicity had only seen grainy newspaper photographs of Agatha on the microfiche in the library. This woman with the hunting knife in her hand must be her prey.

Emma sprang towards her and Felicity shot her in the chest. After Emma had fallen, she coolly fired two bullets into Emma's head.

PC Boyd awoke with a start. A voice on his radio was calling him. "Yes?" he asked.

"Be on the look-out. Emma Comfrey's escaped."

"When?"

"About an hour and a half ago."

"Roger."

And then Boyd heard shots from inside the house. The door was standing open. He rushed in. He saw the woman who had given him the wine standing over a body on the floor. He flung himself on her as she fired and the shot went wild. He pinned her down and got the handcuffs on her.

Then he radioed for help.

As he went outside, his legs were shaking. He was in deep trouble. They would ask how both women had got past him and he would need to say he had been asleep. He pulled a photograph out of his pocket. The woman with the gun was Felicity Felliet and he hadn't recognized her. But, wait a bit, she had that scarf over her head. I bet that wine was drugged, he thought. Please let it be drugged. Of course it was.

The police could not keep Agatha out of the papers after that. All those attempts on her life were headline news. Agatha's first thought was to flee to some hotel and wait till the fuss died down, but then she thought publicity was just what the agency needed, and so she bragged about her prowess on television, on the radio and in the newspapers.

Reading the accounts, Roy and Charles found no mention of their names.

First Charles phoned up and sarcastically asked how it felt to have done it all on her own. Flustered, Agatha began to reply, but then he hung up on her.

Then came Roy at his most waspish. "You've forgotten what it's like to be in PR, you old hag," he said. "Any publicity helps. You seem to want your friends just when you need them and otherwise you're not prepared to help or go out of your way. You're a disgrace!"

Agatha fumed for days. They were both being ridiculous. After all, the solution had been her idea. Anyway, she couldn't spare any time to worry about them. The detective agency was so busy she was having to turn down clients.

Bill Wong called one evening. "Well, it's all sewn up. Felicity was simply using Jeremy and told us all we need to know about him and his operations."

"The thing that puzzles me," said Agatha, "is why he should send a death threat to the daughter he was so fond of?"

"Felicity told us he was prepared to give Cassandra a scare. He said once her mother was shot, she'd soon get over it. I think Jeremy was obsessed with Felicity. When he wound up his import/export agency, he decided it would be better if Felicity took a job abroad so that there would be no connection between the two of them."

"But the police checked out his business. They surely heard about the blonde secretary and wanted to contact her."

"Felicity had been working under an assumed name and papers. She was working under the name of Susan Fremantle. The real Susan Fremantle died last year in a car crash and her home was burgled during the funeral. Jeremy probably bought the papers for Felicity from some villain or other. I'm not quite clear why you managed to jump to the idea that Jeremy had got someone to stand in for him."

"It was one little word—reunion. That's what the French call their AA meetings. The fake Jeremy told the desk clerk that he was going to a reunion. A friend of mine had been talking about some handsome man who had sobered up and from the description it sounded like Jeremy. But it wasn't. I knew Jeremy wasn't an alcoholic, I mean at his age it would have shown on his face and figure."

"You've had all the luck of the amateur," said Bill.

"I," said Agatha Raisin stiffly, "am a professional now."

It was only when the dark days of November began to draw to a close that she began to badly miss Charles and Roy. Business had suddenly gone quiet, as if everyone had decided to save for Christmas, and all the lucrative would-be divorcées planned to leave finding out about their adulterous spouses until after the festive season.

Miss Simms had handed in her notice, saying she was better off at home with her baby daughter because she didn't like leaving her with a baby-sitter the whole time.

Patrick Mullen had suggested Agatha hire a woman detective, Sally Fleming, who had already worked for two other agencies. Sally was small, neat and dark and highly efficient. Instead of the succession of temps, Agatha had also hired a Mrs. Edie Frint as secretary, a widow with impeccable qualifications.

For the first time since she had set up the agency, Agatha had time on her hands and began to mourn her lost friends.

At least there were still Mrs. Bloxby and Bill Wong.

Agatha went along to the vicarage one gusty black November day. She had not told Mrs. Bloxby about the disaffection of Charles and Roy, but now she sought her advice.

"I don't know what to do," wailed Agatha in the comfortable vicarage sitting-room. The log fire crackled and the wind howled around the gravestones in the churchyard. "I thought either of them would have phoned by now."

"Have you tried phoning them?"

"It's no use phoning Charles because that wretched manservant of his is going to say he's not at home even when he is. I tried phoning Roy once, and I could hear his voice in the background, but then his secretary said he was in a meeting."

"Oh dear. Let me think. Are you giving your staff a Christmas party?"

"I thought of a little do in the office, champagne and twiddly bits to eat."

"What about a Christmas dinner at your home? I don't think you've used that dining-room of yours at all. And if you held it, say, two weeks before Christmas, there's a chance both of them might be free of social engagements."

"But why would they come?"

"There's something about the idea of a Christmas dinner that mellows everyone. And I will help you with the cooking."

"That's kind of you. But I'll do it all myself."

"Mrs. Raisin, can you roast a turkey?"

"Any idiot can roast a turkey."

"Not really. We'll talk about it some more. And don't forget to ask Miss Simms."

"All right. But she's not working for me any more."

"But Patrick Mullen is."

"What's that to do with it?"

"Patrick Mullen is Miss Simms's new gentleman friend."

"The sly old dog. Let me see. There'll be Sammy and Douglas, Patrick and Miss Simms, Sally and Edie, Charles and Roy, you and your husband . . ."

"Aren't Sammy and Douglas married?"

"No, neither."

"I'll help you. But it's a terribly busy time of year for Alf and he won't be able to come." Mrs. Bloxby meant her husband would refuse to come.

"Well, that'll be eight, ten including you and me, if you can make it. But this time I am going to do all the cooking."

"And what about Bill Wong?"

"Oh dear." Agatha actually blushed with embarrassment. "What's happening to me? I won't have a friend left if I go on like this."

"Are you really sure you can cope with cooking for all these people?"

"Definitely. It will be a Christmas dinner to remember."

EPILOGUE

†

AGATHA had special invitation cards in red and gold and green printed, asking each recipient to RSVP.

She heaved a sigh of relief when first Roy accepted and then Charles. She had travelled to a turkey farm to choose the largest bird and ordered it to be killed, plucked and hung for several days before delivery.

After studying various recipes for Christmas pudding, she decided it would be safer to buy one. The starter would be simple, smoked salmon wrapped round prawns with a Marie Rose sauce.

The turkey must have all the trimmings—cranberry sauce, sprouts, sweet corn, stuffed mushrooms and gravy. The dining room must be decorated. She must buy really good Christmas crackers. Then should she buy a small present for each guest? Was that going too far? She decided she might as well go the whole hog.

If only the shops weren't so busy. If only that damned Christmas music would stop belting out over the harassed customers. She felt if she heard another rendering of "Have Yourself a Merry Little Christmas" she would scream. The song sounded in her ears like a sneer.

Then there was the Christmas tree which she lugged home, only to find it too tall for the low-beamed ceiling of the dining-room. She sawed the top off and it looked exactly like a Christmas tree with the top sawn off. She threw it into the garden and went and bought another and then spent a whole evening decorating it with golden bows and pretty glass balls. She woke during the night to the tinkle of breaking glass and rushed down to the dining-room.

Hodge and Boswell were happily batting the ornaments with their paws and watching as they dropped to the ground and shattered. She shouted at both of them and the alarmed cats ran up the tree, which keeled over and fell with a crash to the floor.

The next day, Agatha had to go out and buy new ornaments and enlist Doris Simpson's help in cleaning up the mess the cats had made. Then Agatha began to sense—an unusual sensitivity in her case—that Doris was hurt that she had not been invited to the dinner.

Agatha darted through to her desk, where she had fortunately two spare invitations, and quickly penned in Doris's and her husband's names.

"Oh, Doris," she said. "I am so sorry. I forgot to put these in the post!" And she handed Doris the cards.

Doris's face lit up with delight. "That's ever so kind of you. Of course we'll come."

Once the tree was redecorated, with green and silver and red chains decorating the rest of the room, Agatha thought the rest of the house looked bare in comparison. Back to the shops for more decorations.

The turkey was delivered. It was too large to go in the fridge, so Agatha hung it outside the back door. It did not cross her mind that if it was too large for the fridge, it might be too large for her oven.

That was a fact she discovered only on the morning of the dinner party.

She could go and buy another smaller one from the supermarket, but this one was free-range and good quality.

Then she remembered there was a large oven in the kitchen in the village hall. She phoned up Harry Blythe, the chairman of the parish council, and he said, yes, she could use it.

She stuffed the bird, which seemed to take an enormous amount of sausage stuffing. Then she covered the breast with strips of streaky bacon. Finally it was done. She put it in the car and drove to the village hall.

The gas taps on the oven were worn with age and she could not gauge the temperature, so she took a guess.

Agatha slammed the oven door shut just as her mobile phone rang. It was Charles. "Oh, Charles," said Agatha, "I'm so glad you are coming. I thought you'd never speak to me again."

"How many are going to be there?"

"About thirteen of us."

"I hope no one's superstitious. Getting a caterer in?"

"I'm doing all the cooking myself."

"Aggie, are you going to microwave thirteen Christmas dinners?"

"Not a bit of it," said Agatha proudly. "I've this great big fresh turkey. It's so big I had to put it in the oven in the village hall."

"Look, would you like me to come early and help?"

"Thanks, but I can cope."

Agatha returned home and set about preparing the starters on her best china. She had caved in and bought the sauce, so she found the preparation no problem at all. She had already cooked the sprouts, thinking she could heat them up in the microwave. She baked the stuffed mushrooms and then set them aside. They could be warmed up as well.

The kitchen was beginning to look a mess, with dirty dishes and pots and pans.

Agatha decided to go upstairs and change. She put on a long red velvet gown with a slit on one side and very high heels. A gold necklace was the finishing touch.

She went back to the kitchen and tied a long apron over her dress. Surely time to sit down and have a drink. She was feeling exhausted.

Agatha poured herself a large gin and tonic. Then she heard the sound of a siren racing through the village. She stiffened and then relaxed. Everyone who might have threatened her was now dead or locked up.

The phone rang. It was Mrs. Bloxby. "I just called to make sure you were coping all right."

"Fine," said Agatha proudly. "Got everything in hand. The bird was too big for my oven, so I took it up to the oven at the village hall."

"Oh, Mrs. Raisin. Someone just called me and said there was a fire engine at the hall and smoke pouring out of the building."

"Got to go."

Agatha rushed out to her car and drove to the village hall. Harry Blythe was standing outside, looking furious.

He hailed her with "You turned the gas jet too high and that bird of yours began to burn up. The smoke alarms went off and I phoned the fire brigade. It's only smoke, I grant you, but the smoke damage is awful. The walls will all need to be repainted."

"I'll get the decorators in," said Agatha desperately. "What about my bird?"

A fireman emerged from the smoke carrying a roasting pan in his gloved hands. It held a large blackened mound.

Agatha was desperate. She had to stand there and explain herself to the fire chief. She had to mollify Harry Blythe by promising to get decorators in the very next day. Harry began to look almost cheerful. The village hall had been badly in need of redecorating anyway.

"Do you want this?" asked the fireman, holding out the charred turkey.

"No, thank you," said Agatha bleakly. "Throw the damn thing away."

She glanced at her watch. Her guests were due to arrive in an hour.

She went to the delicatessen counter at the general stores and bought up all their sliced turkey. Then she hurried back to her cottage.

She opened the door to the sound of the smoke alarm in the kitchen. The pan of giblets she'd been cooking to make gravy had boiled dry and the stuff was beginning to smoke.

She opened the back door and threw the whole pot out into the garden.

There came a ring at the doorbell. When Agatha opened it,

Charles was standing there. She threw herself into his arms.

"I came early because I thought you'd be making a pig's breakfast of everything. You never could cook."

Agatha drew him into the house, babbling about the ruined turkey.

"What a mess!" said Charles, looking around. "Did you plan to serve that sliced turkey the cats are eating?"

Agatha loved her cats, but right at that moment she felt she could have slaughtered both of them. She chased them out into the garden and sat down and buried her head in her hands.

"Leave it to me," said Charles. "Just come through with your credit card when I call you. Have you got anything to start them off?"

Agatha opened the fridge and pointed. "That looks all right," said Charles. "Go and wipe the soot off your face."

Agatha repaired her make-up and came down the stairs just as the first guests started to arrive.

She poured them all drinks and stood chatting, wondering what Charles was up to.

She went into the kitchen once, but he was on the phone and broke off to say, "Serve them their starters. I'll be in in a moment."

Agatha led them all through to the dining-room. What a terrible expense all this had turned out to be. She had even bought extra chairs for the dining-room. They all exclaimed over the decorations. The table was looking fine. It was decorated with holly wrapped round the base of three tall candles and with her best crystal glasses at each place.

When she went back to the kitchen, Charles had all the starters laid out on three trays.

"Start carrying," he ordered.

Agatha could hardly enjoy the first course, wondering what Charles had arranged to replace the missing turkey. Suddenly, the Christmas carols which had been playing softly in the background started to blast out as the volume increased.

"Excuse me." Agatha got to her feet and hurried out to the kitchen. Men in white coats were carrying large containers into the kitchen.

"Get your credit card," said Charles. "You've got to pay for this."

Agatha meekly paid up without even looking at the bill.

A large golden-brown turkey emerged from its thermal container and was placed on a serving plate. Then came bowls of sprouts, cranberry sauce, mushrooms, peas, roast potatoes, sweet potatoes, warm rolls and a jug of gravy.

"Take the turkey through," ordered Charles, "and I'll bring the rest."

"Did you turn up the volume on the stereo?"

"It was to cover the arrival of this lot at the back door. I'll turn it down when they've left."

Agatha carried the turkey in to the oohs and aahs of her guests. Then she helped Charles carry in the other dishes and turned down the stereo after the last white-coated figure has disappeared.

Roy Silver was wearing a green velvet suit and had a wreath of plastic holly on his head. "Do you forgive me, Roy?" whispered Agatha.

"A meal like this and I'll forgive you anything. Don't do it again."

Agatha began to relax but was aware of Charles's cynical eyes on her each time one of her guests praised her cooking.

The turkey was delicious. Agatha wondered where Charles

had got it from. She had been too upset to read the name on the bill.

"Have you got Christmas pudding?" asked Charles.

"Yes. Don't worry. I bought it. I didn't make it."

"Good, nothing can go wrong then."

Agatha smiled at him fondly. Dear Charles. Roy would be staying over, so Charles could sleep with her that night. She forgot about her vow to forgo casual sex. It was not the sex she wanted but someone to hold her.

Charles and Roy helped her to clear the plates away. "Now, off you go back to the table and I'll bring in the pudding," said Agatha. She took two dishes of brandy butter and a large jug of double cream out of the fridge. "If you'll just take these with you."

"Our Mrs. Raisin's come along no end," said Doris Simpson. "I never would have guessed she could cook like that. Did you know there was some sort of fire up at the village hall?"

"Hasn't burnt down, I hope?" said Roy.

"No, but it seemed someone was using the big oven and burnt something by turning the gas too high. I've told them and told them they ought to paint numbers on the knobs on that old cooker."

Roy's eyes gleamed with sudden malice. "You don't know who was responsible, do you?"

"Not yet. But everyone in the village will know by the morning."

In the kitchen, Agatha took the pudding out of the microwave and tipped it out of its plastic bowl onto a soup plate.

Now to pour brandy over it and light it. No, she would light it at the table. First she carried through the pudding bowls. Would there be enough pudding to go round? Maybe if she did not have any herself.

Then Agatha found to her dismay that she was out of brandy. She searched among the liquor bottles. There was an over-proof bottle of vodka she had brought back from Poland after one of her holidays. That would surely do. All that was needed was a festive blaze.

She poured nearly the whole bottle over it and placed it on a tray with a box of kitchen matches and then carried the tray into the dining-room and set it on the sideboard.

Agatha lifted the pudding off and put it at her place at the head of the table. She fetched the kitchen matches and stood poised.

"Merry Christmas, everyone!" she cried. She struck a match.

She leaped back as with a *whoosh* a great sheet of flame shot up from the pudding. Patrick ran to the kitchen and came back with a fire extinguisher and covered both the pudding and Agatha with foam.

Suddenly everyone began to laugh. Roy started with a high cackle, then Bill Wong, and then the whole table was in an uproar.

Agatha's Christmas party was voted the biggest success ever.

Charles did not stay and Agatha was relieved. It would have been pleasant to go to bed with him, but she knew she would suffer from self-recrimination the day after.

Roy found the bill on the kitchen table as he was helping her to clear up. "You faker," he crowed. "Eight hundred pounds! That bird should have been gilt-edged."

"I never knew it was that much," gasped Agatha. "And now I've got to get the village hall redecorated."

"Never mind. I'll never forget that Christmas pudding. What kind of brandy did you put on it?"

"It wasn't brandy. I'd run out. I poured practically a whole bottle of vodka I brought back from Poland a couple of years ago."

"That stuff! You might as well have used petrol."

"I know. I know. Gosh, I'm exhausted."

Tinkling sounds of breaking glass came from the dining-room. "Oh, Lord," said Agatha. "I forgot to shut the dining-room door and the cats are wrecking the tree. I'll let them get on with it. I'm too tired to move."

"Off to bed with you," said Roy. "We'll clear up in the morning."

"Doris is coming to help me. It'll be all round the village in the morning about that burnt turkey. I didn't tell you about that, did I?"

"I guessed the minute I heard. Off to bed."

Agatha rose and winced as she felt that pain in her hip. It couldn't be anything serious. She was too young. Early fifties these days *was* young.

"The villagers will be even more hostile towards me," said Agatha as she made for the stairs. "I didn't notice until recently and Mrs. Bloxby told me it was because they blamed me for bringing all this murder and mayhem to the village. I might have to move."

"Nonsense. You belong here."

Agatha phoned a firm of decorators and accepted their horrendous charge, saying she would pay their bill if they started immediately.

She went down to the general stores to buy the Sunday papers and was greeted on all sides by friendly smiles and greetings such as "Morning, Mrs. Raisin. Bit nippy this morning."

She bought the papers and returned to her cottage to find Mrs. Bloxby waiting for her. "Come in," said Agatha. "The kitchen's a mess. Roy's here but he hasn't woken up yet and Doris should be along shortly to help. The villagers seem to have thawed towards me."

"They're all laughing about your burnt turkey. Every housewife who's ever messed up a meal is in sympathy with you, and then everyone likes a good laugh."

"I may stay after all."

"You weren't thinking of leaving, were you?"

"It had crossed my mind."

"Nonsense. Believe me, you will never be involved in such a horrendous set of murders or attempted murders again."

But Mrs. Bloxby was wrong.